MW00377573

Copyright © 2022 Matthew Glasgow

All rights reserved

The characters and events portrayed in this book are fictitious. Any similarity
to real persons, living or dead, is coincidental and not intended by the author.

No part of this book may be reproduced, or stored in a retrieval system,
or transmitted in any form or by any means, electronic, mechanical,
photocopying, recording, or otherwise, without express written permission
of the publisher.

ISBN: 9798649331876

Cover design by: Matthew Glasgow
Library of Congress Control Number: 2018675309
Printed in the United States of America

NON EXCIDET

He Will Not Fail

Matthew Glasgow

Non Excidet by Matthew Glasgow

The murky liquid glided and gushed endlessly; a sliver of incandescence breaking through the oppressive fog to create the faintest glisten on the obsidian waves. The abyss covered the whole of the earth. Not dead. Not born. An utterly peaceful nothingness.

Deep down the cascading blackness, at the bottom of the earth, rested a single cell in the consuming depth. Above, a fantastic illumination pierced through the dark, lurching and swaying until it was flush with the cell, closer, closer, and it was soon to be that the cell was not alone in the nothingness, and there were two.

CHAPTER ONE

The female peered out into the light while nursing her child, and the male gathered his pack and set out for the hunt. In the male's heart, there was a burn for the female. He burned for the pleasure to come after the hunt, the caress and the last burst of energy, the meal, if the hunt was successful, finished, the light vanishing from the sky, and the moment he could close his eyes. His burn was also for the required energy, his utter dependence on other for life. She had it within her. She shared it with the child. Ah, but I do truly create the life, he thought further, for without my hunt, her breasts would run dry.

He entered the woods, the darkness, crouching past the tender leaves which he had learned from his elder as a boy not to consume. He did not believe his elder, and tasted the leaf one hot light. It had illed him greatly, and he could not journey with his elder until the light returned twice more. Remembering this time, he now gazed at the leaf with bitterness of taste and feeling. It meant another light of the hunt and not the effortless pluck and consumption at his fingertips.

He crept farther into the darkness, the sharpened bone in his hand. The darkness could give, or it could take. A wise hunter could feed his kin for a life, or it could take the hunter, and after a time, the kin would perish. It had taken his elder, and his male kin, in his burn, rushed into the darkness before the next light, and was taken by it as well. He tried to vanish this thought often, for a clouded hunter would easily be taken, but it always returned, as the light returned with each sleep.

As he stepped, he spotted a flesh from the corner of his eye and bludgeoned the sharpened bone to the earth. As he lifted his tool, he realized the flesh contained no meat and was coarse and dry as a stick, yet limp. This had been prey, but long since dead. As he continued, he marked a rustle in the darkness. Prey! Rabbit, jumping in a fury!

He threw his tool toward the meat, but the meat skipped away, seeming to not notice the sharpened bone nearly hit its long ears. The male leaped to retrieve his tool and continue the pursuit. The rabbit was, fortunately, bounding toward the clearing, where the darkness was bisected by the light above. The rabbit then stopped, oscillating its head until it finally spotted the male. With his tool arched behind his head, the male gathered his strength for the throw. "My light, my guide," he said to himself and tossed the tool once more. This time it had soared well over the rabbit's head and somewhere into the darkness. Defeated, he trudged towards the tool, the rabbit still, mocking, ready to sprint away if the male came within proximity, when suddenly an arm-shaped object sprang from the darkness and pulled the rabbit away.

Frightened, the man dug another tool from his pack and assumed the hunter's stance. He had now become the rabbit, head moving in all directions at the cruel darkness. He heard the rustle once again, but the location seemed omnipresent. He would turn left, and he heard it from the right. He would turn right, and he heard it at his back. Suddenly, the arm darted out again, and the male wildly slashed. He felt blade against meat and withdrew his tool, which now had a splattering of blood. The arm was a creature which moved on its stomach. Its eyes pierced the male like a first cut on the finger from when the hunter tests the tool's sharpness. The creature lighted from above, the whole of the rabbit in its mouth, the incision on the other end. The creature, in almost a sign of triumph and glory, then swallowed the rabbit down its throat, which is all the creature appeared to be, and then swerved back down into the darkness. The male was baffled. Not only had the tool not killed the creature, the creature had the strength to continue its meal!

The man had little luck in his hunt that light, and only killed two rabbits for the female and child. His mind wandered to thoughts of this creature, this beast. No, not a beast. It was a true hunter. Cunning, ruthless, and proud of the prey it killed. It was unlike the large beasts, larger and stronger than the male, with sharp, myriad teeth and claws. Those, they were beasts, for there was no true strategy, just brute force. This creature, this hunter, hid, waited, and struck with precise viciousness, and it took all that was his.

As the lights passed, the male found himself back in the darkness, again after his prey. He heard a beast's roar in the distance and quickened his pace. The terrain had been rough and almost completely untrodden, and he tactfully maneuvered over stones, twigs, and bushes. While passing, he felt a fur and instinctively swung his tool. To his dismay, the fur did not budge, so he bent down and picked it up. The fur, once in the light, had the markings he had known, the tethers for carry and storage, the bloods from the hunts. It was the pack of his elder.

He walked farther, as the roar came nearer--its location imperceptible to the male. Memory of the elder entered his mind once again. The elder told of deep waters, the earth consumed in wave until the light appeared and the waters were dried. The elder said he had not witnessed it with his own eyes, but he knew it to be true.

The male reached the waters, exiting the darkness to relieve his thirst. As the male drank, he saw motion in the waters; he saw the great beast. Its gaze, however, was not on the male, but something below its feet. It roared and unsheathed its teeth and lunged toward the earth. However, instead of picking its head up to reveal the bloody prey in its jaw, it yelped and scampered away.

The male saw the earth move, and the long-arm creature, the true hunter, emerged. It had not only survived the male's laceration lights prior, it had seemingly grown back the part of its arm that was cut off! The male walked through the water to approach the creature, which was taut from the beast's attack. As it moved, it shed a layer of its flesh, as if birthing itself. The male stood in awe, eyes locked with this fantastic creature. Suddenly, he heard a roar from the darkness, and the beast returned. It snarled and breathed heavily, its tongue wagging rhythmically. The male looked into the beast's eyes and did not see fury, but fear, and in that instant the beast collapsed to the earth, revealing the creature's bite mark, bloody, symmetrical circles, on its hind leg. The beast let out a heavy breath and was dead. Its meat could feed the male, female, and male child for many lights.

The female soon had another child, a female also, and soon another male. The female nursed and gave life to the little ones, and the male continued to hunt, yet as he went into the darkness, he thought of this long-arm creature, whom he named serpent, and asked it to guide him in catching his prey. It had taught him to hunt with more precision; it had provided him with sustenance, as he would find other dead beasts with the circle markings, yet he also knew to step lightly, as the same blow could be rendered to him if he angered this creature.

As the eldest male grew older, the male took him out to the hunt. Before entering the darkness, the elder male told his child of the serpent, and the two males asked for its guidance. The two males hunted together, and as the lights passed, the child soon became a skilled hunter. The elder too felt more capable with each light, and caught meat nearly every time in the woods.

While hunting with the child one light, the pair saw a shadow move through the stones by the waters. Instinctively, the two raised their tools for the prey or the fight. The creature soon emerged from the stones and meandered toward the elder and child. The elder, upon recognizing the serpent, lowered his tool. It had guided him well through the lights, and he believed it would not do him harm. The serpent continued to move forward, its eyes sharp and its hiss hypnotic. The child, who had not known the serpent as the elder had, kept his tool raised. To the child, it was beast, but looking at his father's gentle stance, he was not sure.

The serpent moved forward; its sound almost saying its name, which the elder had given it. The child was told, but knew not of this beast's guidance. He only saw the sharp of its eyes and teeth. His elder said that though its teeth were small, they could bring down the mightiest of beasts.

"Guide. Guide," the elder spoke softly and closed his eyes as the serpent was nearly at his feet. It opened its mouth wider, teeth glistening from the light, and raised its head to the male. "Yes," the elder spoke and opened his eyes to see into those of the serpent.

The elder stood, awaiting a reply by the great being, when the child swung his tool down on the serpent, severing its head.

In silence, the two stood, both waiting for the creature's head to grow back on its body. As the light began to vanish, the elder finally knelt down and held the serpent's limp body in his hand and wept.

The lights passed, and the hunts continued. The eldest male grew stronger with each light, and he was soon a master hunter. The elder and male spoke little of the day the serpent left, only that it would return one day as long as the males continued to give it reverence. The young male would nod solemnly to the elder's words on the serpent, but deep down, he did not truly believe. To the young, the serpent was a mere creature, meat and--if anything--foe, not friend or guide. The elder knew of the child's thought. The child heard but did not listen. And, it had been the child's fault that the serpent departed! These thoughts made the burn come back to the elder.

The female soon revealed to be with another child as her stomach grew with each light. The female spoke very little, but always had a smile upon her face as she looked down on her offspring. She births and nurses, the elder thought, but I mold. The eldest male child can hunt as well, if not better than I, and we keep the kin fed. Although the serpent has left us, I continue to ask for his guidance, and we continue to thrive until we are ready for him to come back again. With two fingers, he drew the winding serpent in the sand.

The male would have the look in his eyes that would often cause her to lie awake as the light left. Her male elder had it, her male kin had it as well. The males went into the darkness, spilled the blood of the prey and carried its meat, yet still had a burn, beyond the need for her flesh, which frightened plenty, but was much more dangerous. It came in small moments: a sharp reprimand while she nursed her young, a hand raised as she gathered his pack and tool, a bellow that "the hunt was his, not hers", coursing veins across taught tendons. He knew so very little, they, the males, knew so very little, and deep down, they truly knew it as well, as the male wandered to the hunt and the female gave life.

The elder and his eldest child walked in the darkness, early in the hunt. The elder, seeing that his child was nearly a full male, now often spoke of kin, as his time waned and his hunt not as strong. As they trudged in the darkness this day, he heard the beast's roar on the hill and steadied their tools--now sharper and more vicious as the child learned to magnificently articulate the bone of the tool into a cutting blade. The pair deftly stepped from the beast's roar, but another beast's roar trapped the two hunters. The woods soon crashed in the darkness, and the pair tumbled forward, blind to the valley at their feet. The elder tossed over twigs and stones, lacerating his hands and breaking bone in his knee. He wheezed as he reached the valley's nadir, broken and awaiting the darkness to take him as it had his kin before him. Groping in the darkness, the child found his elder and leaped on his prone, severed body as the beast pursued. The child heard the beast's nostrils as it came within a hair's length of the two hunters. Closing his eyes, the child thought "serpent, guide." The beast then passed into the darkness and the child carried the elder's body into the light.

The elder slept long, missing the hunt for several lights. The female kept vigil, and it was soon that the elder was like one of her children. His breath was faint, and his only noises were of pains deep within his body, sounding like the beasts of the darkness and light's end. He finally opened his eyes after many lights and tried to rise, only to fall back to the earth. There he stayed, bound to the earth until the light was at its end and the elder saw his child return with several meats of prey slung to his shoulder. The child had done well, and the kin, the elder included, ate well that evening.

Some strength returned to the elder, but he still could not

stand, and by no means join in the hunt. As the male sat with the female, he began to speak more prevalently. He spoke of light after he would pass, and what his kin would do once he was gone. Only such thoughts seemed to be in his head since he had fallen during the hunt. The female knew not of the wonders of the serpent, nor the true skill of the hunt, and he began to tell her and the other children many tales. His kin sat in quiet awe of the elder, and the elder began to see their belief in the serpent and the hunt as well. The elder thought that "male" and "female" would no longer be sufficient. For when he would leave and the female and children too, who would remember of their time but the earth and sky? He named himself Ahk, and he named the female Ur. His children, the eldest male would be Ahk-Yon, the female child, Ur-Yon, and the youngest male, Ahk-Ser.

Ahk grew strong enough to stand, but pain would soon pull his knees to the earth, and his hands had strength to hold, but not to strike; he would continue to be left from the hunt. Ahk-Yon ensured him that the serpent would guide and allow his bones to heal, as it had done to itself. Ahk smiled, as he knew his child now believed.

One light as he hunted, Ahk-Yon saw the serpent reappear, now in the path which had been an untrodden clearing. The light shimmered on its head and its piercing eyes enraptured Ahk-Yon. "Please, great guide, heal my elder as you do yourself. Give new life as it comes to you!" Ahk-Yon spoke. The serpent remained unmoved, yet Ahk-Yon heard the serpent's voice from behind him. Ahk-Yon peered into the darkness until the serpent crawled out and joined Ahk-Yon on the path. How could this be, Ahk-Yon thought as he snapped his head back and forth. Two serpents? He heard the hiss louder, and soon two more serpents emerged, followed by two more, and soon he was surrounded.

The hiss nearly deafened him, but he did not shut his ears. Perhaps they were giving him a message; he needed to endure the hissing sting longer. The serpents continued to move closer and soon formed a circle around Ahk-Yon. Their eyes all gazed upon him sharply. He had known such looks from the beasts of the darkness. He took out his tool and rotated himself while in the serpent circle. As one leapt toward his face, Ahk-Yon swung fiercely and continued to swing until he was released from the scaley tethers. He ran up the path but glanced back to view several lifeless serpents on the trodden earth.

He had not the courage to tell the elder of the event in the darkness. The elder's health in body did not return, but with each light, he seemed more enveloped in this serpent and his own tales. Ahk-Yon noticed the tales begin to change; even the times he had experienced with the elder seemed grander, with larger beasts, rougher terrain, and the omnipresent aid from the serpent.

Ur's stomach grew during this time, and as the darkness sifted from the skies, she birthed another female, and she was named Ur-Ser. At the child's birth, Ahk realized that his strength would not return. He watched Ur nurse and smile, and he watched his eldest male, Ahk-Yon, walk to the hunt. He seemed out of tales, and he knew those oldest remembered who he once was, and soon they would all regard him as an old fool. "This can not be, for I am Ahk, and the serpent is my guide."

With the light passing into darkness, Ahk-Yon returned from the hunt with meat for his kin. The settlement was amiss, as Ur was not nursing the female child, Ur-Ser, on the furs of the great beast of the darkness, but rather his elder was holding the child.

"Ahk will live, the serpent will guide," Ahk whispered, rocking the young Ur-Ser back and forth.

"Elder?"

Ahk peered at Ahk-Yon, the burn in Ahk's eyes through the darkness.

"The male creates, the male gives life, the male endures. Ahk, with you too, and your males, and our kin will be great! The darkness no more!" Ahk screamed and shook Ahk-Yon. "The lights are there in the sky! Others have been great, and they stay above for all time!"

Ahk-Yon felt the warm liquid on the elder's hands. Blood.

"They," Ahk pointing at Ur-Ser and then in the distance,

"birth, but we can take! Without the take there is no life!"

Tears now entered both males' eyes.

"Ur? No."

"Yes! Yes!"

They collapsed into themselves, down into the cold earth; Ahk-Yon seeing the bloody tool by his elder's side, and they wept.

Ahk-Yon left with Ur-Yon the following light, out past the darkness to where the elder's eyes could not see.

Ahk, carrying Ur-Ser and aided by Ahk-Ser, walked into the darkness, all weary from lack of meat. Ahk stumbled over twigs and stones until his male child guided him to the trodden path. There, they found the dead serpents, many rotted, but one flailing from small lacerations until it at last too was lifeless. Ahk looked at his children and the sky, unsure for a moment, but then realizing, "He has died so we may live," and they ate the serpent.

CHAPTER TWO

The tribe wandered through the desert, free of their captors but in desperate need of food and water. Women and children moaned in agony, and several tribesmen perished with each new day. They had reverted to a previous time, scouring the earth for edible shrubs, vermin, or even large insects. They had eaten in ways that angered their god, and some even questioned His existence. Over dunes and buttes, the head tribesman lead with his staff. He had promised his people freedom, and this, at least, they had. As he heard their cries and felt his own pangs and withering body, he questioned if he had made the right decision. They were slaves, but they were not dead. Had there been a time without such things? Why was God so cruel as to bring suffering and death? Was it better to have independence or a life of servitude?

The days of wandering and suffering continued, and then were the days of the fiery serpents. So wicked was it for a creature to crawl on its belly and strike at man's heels--to forever cause man to look down on the earth, to startle from a sound sleep, to fear. And this serpent was in man too. It was in the pyramid builders and bronze shapers and men-enslavers. To kill and punish without mercy so they can survive. Not only a survival of a man's life, but to live on beyond that. To be a statue or a tale enscripted in the stone. The head tribesman even knew these serpents were within his own people. Could it even be within himself?

The serpents who crawled through the sand afflicted his people with much death. His people reached to the sky and cursed their vengeful god. He knew their anger, and it angered him as well. "You live or you die! It is not your role to question His decision! He brings this creature to us as another test! It is in our suffering that we have our faith!" The tribeman looked among his people. "Melt your brazen chains and create a serpent of bronze. It is only through praising our death-bringer that we may live!"

The people constructed the brazen snake and nailed it to a staff. They were then never struck by the serpents until they found their way home.

CHAPTER THREE

Eusebius passed by Saint Peter's Basilica, stopping for a moment to marvel at the impressive structure. It had once been a circus during the time of Nero. The emperor had gone mad with the potential glory he could achieve for himself and Rome; his mind diluted by ancient kings like Priam and the sensational plays of Greece. He set his city ablaze in hopes of clearing the old structures for his new grand design and golden kingdom. As the fire eventually burned out, he blamed the upstart disciples of Christ and performed public martyrdoms on his circus. Peter, Christ's disciple, was said to have fled the city when Christ appeared to him and said to Peter that he, Christ, had returned to be martyred again. It was then that Peter, the one who had lost his faith on the water and sank, and who denied knowing Christ to save himself from death, and had tried for the remainder of his life to atone for this sin by making others have faith and have the courage to say they know Christ and accept their own martyrdom for the Kingdom of God with faith that they will live again, finally completed his covenant by taking the cross for Christ and dying on Nero, the matricidal thespian and emperor's grounds. It was with the martyrdoms for life again that the followers of Christ continued to grow while Nero eventually fled to the hills and opened his veins and knew it was his duty to do so. Peter's body was placed in the catacombs of Nero's circus, and soon the tomb became a place of pilgrimage, then a shrine, and now a basilica commissioned by the emperors of Rome themselves.

Eusebius continued down the street until he reached the market. There he purchased a bottle of wine and seared steak and made his way to the opium hall. A senator was oratting on a precipice by the state building about the continued need for piety in order to maintain the glory of the empire. While the plutarchs and plebeians and slaves applauded alike, Eusebius scoffed at the senator's cliched and clunky rhetoric and continued on his way. He had won much favor by his schoolmaster because of his oration skills, but more importantly his mastery of language, both Latin and Greek. It was now nundinae, market day, and he longed to put the studies of language and old Greek tragedies aside and consume in all of the pleasures of life. That was what those Christians did not understand, he thought while drinking his wine in the hall and watching his opium pipe burn. They live just to deny the pleasures of the earth! They see not that our own end could be tomorrow, so why not live the best way possible? They deny the plays and poems that give us true feeling--sorrow and joy! Speak and write with precision and elegance, and you will be immortal enough, and live again when someone reads what you have written or remembers what you have said. Live on in the hearts and minds of men.

He continued to drink until he was free of inhibitions. True freedom in his mind. True religion as the spirit and god has taken hold of the flesh. Eusebius went to bed with women of the hall, drank the wine, and consumed the hallucinogens until he was free of memory and was carried home by his comrades.

On Sunday, he walked to the catacombs of the saints and martyrs. His guilt pressed heavily on his mind and coursed through every hair of his being. A collage of memories and sensations seemed sown to his innards and he could not find the thread to unravel them away. He had spoken to his tutors, but they were of little help. They too, embraced the hellenistic pleasures and found no need for regret in fulfilling the cadre of desires in men. Perhaps these catacombs would lead him to some--at least temporary--catharsis.

The catacombs were deep in the earth. Eusebius descended the dark, steep staircase until he reached the crypts with only a torch to light his way through the darkness. There were stone carvings of fish, which Eusebius knew as Christ recruited apostles who were previously fishermen, and crucifixes for their messiah's execution. The dank smell of death was ever present. Bone and flesh rotting away in their stone tombs, some bodies enduring incineration, maulings, decapitations, arrows, and of course, crucifixions. This sacrifice and martyrdom enraptured Eusebius's mind. They had died for their beliefs and had no fear. They talked of a world to come, where God would be with them and they would never die. These beings, shut in their stone cells, would return and have the glory, for they helped give it to themselves. Eusebius stepped farther and saw the relief of Christ as the good shepherd carrying the young lamb on his shoulders. He leaned closer to examine the details of this Christ figure when his torch suddenly blew out. In the darkness, he was alone with his immense grief. His mind raced and he began to think of his own death and the idea of truly being dead and just being bones in a grave and then one day dissolving away and the afterlife and the river Styx and paying the ferryman and Ulysses deep down in the underworld and seeing his mother and then Agamemnon betrayed by his lover and great Achilles who would trade life as a dirt farmer for glory in death and a god coming to Earth and co-mingling with man and man killing god and then denying Him and then for Him to deny you salvation and then his mind stopped. He felt the martyrs and apostles before him and he felt the faith and he knew that anything great was a sacrifice and his pen could lead to their--everyone outside of the catacombs- salvation. So he wrote and denied himself of the pleasures of the Earth and died one day in a cave in Bethlehem, a hermit and transcriber of the sacred text.

CHAPTER FOUR

He was awakened by a stiff jab to the stomach by one of the clan's oarsmen. He had slept since they chained him and threw him in the ship's hold. His father was a tax collector, so the clan assumed they could plunder the family's estate, but the dilution of wealth and power from the Romans and rumors of sackings by the Vandals and other clans left simply no money for his father to collect on the whole British island. Patricius wondered how these pirates of King Niallach knew of his family's estate. Was it skill of the raider, or had his father's taking of other's money prompted an enemy to sell him out. To some, it made no difference if it was called plunder or tax, and they probably thought he got what he deserved. These pirates came in the night, set the cottage house on fire, killed or captured the swine, emptied his father's coffers, and beat him and his family before dragging him, Patricius, onto the ship. For all he knew, his father and mother were likely killed. These clansmen of the kingdom of Ulster and the Irish island were those of legend and nightmare. They had swept through the lands for centuries, plundering, raping, and murdering, stiking unexpectedly, venomously, and without mercy. The clan names changed often, but the names did not matter. He did not believe in Christ like his father, but he did believe in the evils of the Earth. These clansmen were that evil, that looming sword that comes in the night. Not merely of vengeance or property or wealth, but of the pure animalism in man. The need for survival and the deep down knowledge that the biggest threat out there for survival is man itself. So, the choices are to be the bearer of the sword in the night, or to be the one sleeping, dreaming of a nightmare that will one day be true, and maybe never even waking to see that it has been realized and become flesh.

His father gifted him a copy of the Latin transcribed Bible day before, when he turned sixteen. It had always grieved his father that Patricius did not share in the faith or believe in Christ, and this book, bound finely and written by an elegant hand, signified his final effort, his last act in trying to save his son's soul. Now, it was Patricius's only possession, which he tactfully hid under his tunic and away from the pirates' greedy hands.

The ship rocked violently along the ocean, and its creaks and bellows made Patricius think that it would snap in two at any moment. The thought did not worry him; he would soon be dead or enslaved once they reached land anyway. The ship's hold was utter darkness save a few cracks in between the wood panels revealing endless ocean and fog. He could hear the other captives breathing heavily and readjusting their shackles, but he, nor any of them, spoke a word. There were three types of men in the world: free men, slaved men, and dead men. It seemed that a man lived as all three at one time or another, and often envied the man he was not. This book under his tunic spoke of chosen men and those whom God spoke to, and now the son of God whom the Romans crucified some four hundred years ago. Man was so unimaginably cruel to think of such things--to hold dominion over all living things of the Earth, and then the people of the Earth whom you conquer and who believe differently and come from different clans so you kill and annihilate until that people is no more or they are in chains to tend the earth you have claimed is yours and pluck the grains and herd the swine and sheep and then you tell the one in chains to serve you in battle and they die graveless or if they just survive just to return home for you to kill on a day you see fit because they are yours just like the animals you feed scraps to and fatten up until they are no longer of use so you slaughter them for your banquet halls while other kings drink your wine and are to numb to even taste the meats and have your women or you kill the animal for your god and it is a sacrifice for you loved that animal but that animal who served you well and never ran from your field and licked your toes never truly wanted that life and would have been better off cold and hungry and dying in the teeth of a great wolf than to be confined to the fields you have won through spilling man's blood.

The ship arrived on the Irish coast on a foggy, gray morning. Patricius and the other captives were herded up the rocky shoreline through the bog and into the oak forest until they reached the cave of the Druids. The cave was lined with vines and thin trees weaved as in a fabric or woman's hair, painted in mauve, ochre, and emerald. Atop the cave's entrance hung a large, wooden sun--its face of a dire man with a heavy beard and piercing eyes. The Druid high priest emerged from the cave with an iron staff in his hand. He spoke to the priests in the Gaelice tongue, which Patricius could vaguely comprehend, and the pirates seized a captive, a muscular young man, who from his build, may have been a Roman soldier, and escorted him to a large granite rock in a clearing feet from the Druid cave. Three other Druid priests appeared in this clearing, adorned with silk robes of dark blue and wearing crowns of laurel on their heads. The pirates laid the captive on the slab and held him down; the captive wailing out and vowing the his people would have their vengeance on King Niallach, the pirates laughing maniacally at his threats. The high priest walked to the slab, humming in a low octave and holding his staff in one hand and a dagger in the other. At the foot of the slab, he looked to the sky and said, "For our kingdom, our prosperity, and peace, we give you this strong youth. It is only in sacrifice that we can all live." He then held the dagger to the sky, turned the blade downward, and stabbed it into the captive's stomach. The captive cried out into the silent forest and the priest moved the blade up to his chest and pressed the blade farther down. Blood ran down the youth's convulsing body and onto the slab; the other priests standing motionless. The pirates slowly released their grip on his body and in another moment the convulsing ceased and it was finished.

Patricius was taken to King Niallach's castle, which was high on the hill overlooking the oak forest. There, he was given wine and cooked lamb until he was full. Niallach appeared after the captives had their meals and stood before Patricius and the others. He was tall and had a wide, muscular form from his days of war, but beginning to fatten since becoming king. He was bald and had a long beard which was still red along his cheeks but white around his mouth and chin. Niallach wore a brazen chest plate with an oak tree carved in the middle and the same image of the anthropomorphic sun above the oak. He wore a black robe of coarse wool with wolf's fur along the collar, and his crown was gold and jeweled. Niallach unsheathed his sword from his hip, held it to the castle ceiling, and then pointed it to the captives.

"You Britons have been brought to my kingdom, entered my home, and ate and drank of my finest substances, for I and my people, aside from what they may say, are not barbarians. We do not build monuments to the gods or great kings or write down the word, for we are a humble people, and we do not delight in decadence. We are a people of one. We are one family and our actions are driven towards the survival of our family and not some individual fame or glory. We have taken you from your lands because you are needed. We need you for our fields and for our sheep and swine. We need you for your sword if the day shall ever come. We need your sacrifice. From this day on, do not think of yourselves as captives or slaves, think of yourselves as gods, as the holiest ones among us. Serve your sacrifice well and you will not fall under the yoke of the whip by your master, but kissed and loved and fed the goods of the earth. Go now, you holy men, for your sacrifice awaits."

Patricius was taken to the marketplace, where he was auctioned off for servitude. Wealthy landowners barked prices as Patricius stood on the block. One laughed at his lanky frame and his hands, which were soft and did not show the marks of hard labor. "A rich boy!" the man concluded, "He will die in the fields as his brow feels its first drop of sweat!" Patricius stood quietly until the bickering ended and an old landowner named Barra stepped up and purchased him for half of what was asked.

Patricius was taken to Mount Slemish to herd Barra's swine. He was renamed Magunus, or servant lad, and Barra would call him Sochet, or swineherd, when he was doing his work. During his first few days, he was defiant, and refused to listen to his command. Barra, even at his old age, had impressive strength and would beat Patricius bloody with his bare fists, and when he tired, he would take up his walking stick and bludgeon Patricius as well. Patricius still refused, thinking death would be more suitable than a life of servitude. He was refused food and drink, and chained to a post in the slave quarters. Beaten and hungry, he stared out into the clover fields and sheep trodding along as the sun faintly glimmered through the fog. This clover was myriad and indomitable. As often as it was cut down or pulled from the earth, it only returned, and often greater in strength. He had submitted himself to death since his capture, but he was still here. Something had kept him here and not dead in the night. He would fight another day, and do as they asked in the interim.

His first days as a herdsman did not go well. Patricius was unfamiliar with the lands and rule, and was almost beaten by another herdsman when he led his flock of swine through the peat of another landowner. Patricius had difficulty wrangling the swine as well, and in the first week, he had lost three and was whipped for the failure. Now he did not protest; he just hung his head and endured the scourge.

He improved over the weeks and he soon had the skill to lead the flock through the highlands of Antrim and down into the lowlands and into the market. He found that he was adept at selling the swine to townspeople, and he began to make a good profit for Barra. "It is the lad's education," Barra would say. "He knows the word as the priests know the word."

As the success continued for Patricius, Barra gifted him finer robes, gave him the prime cuts of meat and the smoothest wine, and no longer whipped or beat him. Barra then moved him to shepherd as profit would be consistent for the wool over several seasons until the animal could be used for meat.

Being a shepherd was a lonely profession for Patricius, as he spent his days with his flock and spent his nights in a small cabin on a hill by himself. After the sheep had their exercise and fodder for the day, Patricius would eat his meal and sit by the hearth, thinking of home and the reality of a lifetime in this alien land. He thought of escape often, as he now was away from the watch of Barra, but he knew he could not go far without being spotted, and he had no boat to leave the island. To pass the time, he would read the Bible his father had given him, and found a bond with the people of Abraham and their plight. They were placed in bondage, as he had been, they had the courage to escape, they wandered through the desert with a burning goal for home, risking suffering and death for the hope of freedom. The book showed the evils of man--avarice, oppression, lust, and wrath--but also the mercy and forgiveness--the beauty of man to truly do for another. In the despair of his slavery, Patricius fixated on the lines spoken by Jesus, "Come to me, all of you who labor and are burdened, and I will give you rest. Take my yoke upon you and learn from me, for I am meek and humble of heart, and you will rest for yourselves. For my yoke is easy, and my burden light." Patricius thought of his own burden and the cruelty he had faced. He also considered his parents or others who met a worse fate than he, like the captive cut open on the slab. His desire for freedom never waned, but he found through prayer his worry and anger subsided, and he focused on his flock.

Patricius walked on nearly every blade of grass, pebble or grain of sand of Ireland over the next six years. He loved his flock and found himself immensely intrigued with Jesus as the good shepherd. He mourned whenever a sheep went missing and rejoiced when it was found. He cared for their coats, and they often ate better than he. Patricius had even fended off salivating wolves on several occasions.

Roaming the country, he felt he knew almost all on the island. They were good people deep down, but they were infected by these pagan gods and the secretive priests of the forest, as well as the constant threat of war through Niallach's ruthless campaigns. Niallach and the kings of the island lusted for the material of the world--gold, jewels, herbs, beer and wine--and they forced the humble farmer or artisan to take up arms and raid or shed blood just for further goods of no real purpose but lust and temporary euphoria. If the people were to sacrifice, it should be pure in the denial of wants of the Earth. Only by fully denying the materials that lead to sin could a person be cleansed and forge a kingdom that God would walk in again. From this perspective, his servitude was closer to a calling from God. He lived not to hurt or maim or push or pull for gold coins or a family's notoriety or honor with the king. His peace was simply with tending his sheep, reading his scripture, and praying for guidance above.

He believed he reached such guidance one cool autumn evening as he was awakened from the winds crashing against his cottage on the hill. The room had a divine illumination and a voice, resonant and sweet, said to him, "Leave this house. Run to the sea. There, a boat will be waiting for you to take you home."

Just as soon as it had appeared, it left Patricius. He stood dumbfounded, and thought it all may have been the fog of a dream, or the loneliness, or a wild herb that blurred his mind. Nevertheless, he had felt it in his heart; a stinging belief that coursed through every fiber like a potent cup of wine or a submersion in ice cold water or the first strike of the whip on your bare back. He knew it was time to journey, and he prayed he would not stray. Patricius gathered his provisions in his shepherd's bag, kissed each sheep of his flock, and set out for the darkness of the oak forest.

He carried a small torch through the night; each crack or hiss or caw or chirp amplified in the blackness and halting him where he stepped. Patricius walked nearly blind through the oak. He heard wolves or possibly bears in the distance, and more violent thrashing from the bushes and branches above. There were legends of wild men of the woods who could see through the darkest night and kill an unsuspecting traveler with machine-like precision. Townsfolk even talked of the spirits of the dead, if not the actual corpses themselves, would roam through the oak in the night. Patricius had fear of these great, unknown entities of the darkness, and prayed for courage and strength. As the dawn began to break, his fear was more practical, as an ill-fated spotting by a landowner or crony of Niallach would mean his capture and most likely execution for fleeing.

As the day grew brighter, Patricius found a brook and dipped his head in, cleansing him from the travel thus far and invigorating himself for the journey to come. With the aid of the brook's reflection, Patricius shaved his beard with a blade and cut his hair until he was nearly bald and resembled a nobleman or Irish soldier. He walked through the peat and stone of the island for the day without being detected by a single person. Rationing his food, and hardly stopping for rest, he walked towards the ocean. After about a week's travel, he reached the shores. As was told to him, a single boat bobbed in the harbor and he was on his way back home.

He made his way through the British island until he finally arrived at his family estate. A figure was reaping the wheat on a hill in the distance, and Patricius cautiously walked up the path, the sun shining brightly and making it difficult to discern the figure's face until he, Patricius, was mere feet away. The figure, miraculously, was his father. The two embraced and beheld each other for a long while until his father said simply, "You have returned," and Patricius handed him his Bible and stated, "I have been reborn."

CHAPTER FIVE

Jude O'Rafferty delicately dipped his index and middle finger into the holy water, made the sign of the cross, and entered Saint Patrick's Cathedral. He bowed his head to the figure of Jesus on the crucifix hanging over the Communion table, which was draped in a violet and white satin sheet imprinted with golden Irish crosses, and walked to the pew, genuflected, and knelt to pray. Saint Patrick drove the serpents, as it were, out of the island centuries before, and the Irish people were shown the way. The pagan, hedonistic and indulgent religions were effaced, and the people took Patrick's message of following Jesus's way to heart. A message of sacrificing pleasures and vices of this life in order to live forever in the next life. To create the Kingdom of Heaven on Earth, a kingdom of singular vision and belief in the Holy Trinity, and one day God would return and the sacrifices and belief in Him would yield eternal bliss and happiness in His presence. That was the understanding of the Irish people, so they destroyed the straw effigies and all of the priests of the forest and gathered their brick and mortar and built great cathedrals, like this, Saint Patrick's in Dublin. A house of worship worthy of a god who died for his people and their sins. A house with marble pillars and finely carved naves adorned with the mysteries of Christ and the heaven of God. Pews of the purest wood, shaped by the master craftsman. Stained glass windows of the most brilliant colors. Now the indulgences of the swine kings across the sea left this cathedral empty, with tiles crumbling down from the ceiling, the floor dusty and soiled, with the threat of fines and enslavement, or death, if these Catholics did not attend the church of the king every Sunday; left to choose between the sufferings on earth and the eternal suffering of their souls. The royalty now jostled for power across the sea with Parliament for divine rule, and there was even talk of executing King Charles. The Protestant British were the majority landowners in Ireland, but there were still a few true Gaelic, Catholic Irish like Felim O'Neil who owned plantation grounds and produced economical crops. In closed circles, O'Neil and his kin talked of overtaking the ruling Brits and giving the island back to the Irish. He, Felim, set his sites for Dublin Castle, his plan being to impersonate a roundhead Parliamentarian magistrate sent to change posts due to a royalist overthrow and send the occupying British back to sea, and then to be armed and never have a Brit step on Irish soil again. This plan, God-willing, would invoke no bloodshed, though those cohorts of O'Neil, like O'Rafferty, knew blood would always be needed in such campaigns.

O'Rafferty helped raise O'Neil's stock and harvest the wheat and potatoes, and they were each other's closest friends. They had grown up in the great city of Dublin, watched waves of iron-plated British soldiers and house members shove papers in the faces of illiterate farmers and shepherds, confiscate their goods, and sometimes literally kicked the men and women to the street. Those who resisted were enslaved and sent to the Caribbean islands to till the cane or sugars for the British empire. And then, the cold days set in, and the crop, no matter British or Irish, withered, died, and did not grow again. Famines set in and the people became truly bitter. O'Rafferty's two younger sisters died before their third birthdays, and his mother one day went out in the foggy morning to visit her mother on the edge of town and collapsed and died on the road, carted back to the family house like a dead wild dog that began to rot on the streets. And then, his father fell to the drink and quarreled with O'Neil senior and the other Irish landowners and was eventually hanged after stabbing a Protestant plantation owner at the public house and babbling on about the trinity of the shamrock and Christ's reckoning on the British swine that tainted the land. An orphan at fourteen, O'Rafferty became like a son to O'Neil senior and a brother to

Felim. The family talked bitterly over the British encroachment and the empire's heavy hand; the stripping bare of their religion, and the day when the British would lift the veils of civility and tolerance and simply wipe the Irish and Catholicism off the face of the Earth. O'Neil senior would tell tales of great famines in the past and plagues that would riddle the island. He'd claim it to all be at the hand of the British, be it through supreme planning and execution, or a bumbling, idiotic gentry whose comedy of errors had caused the doom of the island. As O'Rafferty heard this rhetoric through the years on the plantation, he developed an unending rage within, yet suppressing it as memories of his father, unhinged, a boorish creature of emotion on the street, pulsed through his mind and a final image of his father thrashing from side to side as his hands were tied and two British soldiers shoved his head into the noose and he, his father, stiffening his neck and snarling and spitting at the soldiers and shouting in a twisted Gaelic-English tongue so the oppressors and the oppressed could hear alike but the mixture of language sounding like raving nonsense of a town drunkard who could not simply shut his mouth and say yes sir. So instead of gnashing his teeth or stomping the ground or drinking until ephemeral and creature, O'Rafferty simply took his rosary beads out and prayed his Hail Marys until he had touched each bead and completed each mystery. At twenty-one, O'Rafferty married Brigh Cavanagh and settled in a cottage on the edge of the O'Neil plantation. They had two boys and two girls by the time O'Rafferty was twenty-eight years old. Brigh was a devout Catholic, but not in the public, holier-than-thou way. She read the gospels nightly and could recite full parables or miracles verbatim. O'Rafferty truly loved her. She was not some woman to clean the house, cook the food, and rear the children; the two were true partners. At night while the children slept, Brigh would play the guitar and sing sweet melodies to the pale moon as O'Rafferty read the Bible or wrote poetry which she would put to song. Brigh knew the rage that O'Rafferty believed he kept hidden. She saw the hearth coals in his eyes as he sat on the porch while chomping on a twig and moving the rosary beads in his hands. The war and the carnage were forever tethered to his soul, to all men really, no matter how much he talked of Christ or charity or the good of his fellow man and country. He, like the others, saw the alien footprints on his land. The Anglo-Saxon tongue on his Gaelic ears. The iron armor on his Celtic eyes. The blasphemed Eucharist in his emerald mouth. He read and wrote and reaped and sowed with care, and touched little alcohol or herb besides the occasional holiday, but there was something down deep that would be eternally devil and angel. Devil in the lust for blood when property and faith were taken, which he knew would then be family and friend. And angel in that ability to shed away the civility and kindness and generosity to become his own nightmare and demon in order to protect what was his.

O'Neil's plan to overtake Dublin Castle was foiled when two of his conspirators were captured and confessed to the plot. O'Neil, now uncloaked as the rebel ringmaster, knew the time for strategy was at an end. Parliament and Scottish Covenanters threatened to conquer the island and purge all Irish Catholic culture until every soul was aligned to the Church of England. More selfishly, Scots and Brits began to confiscate portions of his land and the land of his father and brothers. He went from cottage to cottage telling the Irish peasants the news of an impending invasion and encouraged all able men in joining the fight. O'Rafferty, of course, was by his side, a man loyal to friend and country, but incredulous as to the reality of this revolution. Could these peasants with corroded swords and pikes stand a chance against the British empire? The magistrates and soldiers that were already on the island could be overthrown, but the British would not relent. They would come with their ships and arms and iron armor and lay waste to the island just to prove a point. However, as O'Neil continued to accrue soldiers, the more O'Rafferty became convinced. These people experienced generations of suffering and servitude, and their hatred and lust for bloodshed was frighteningly real. O'Neil's clan was soon incorporated with Lord Macguire from Antrim, and their rebel army was nearly 10,000 strong. They overtook Dunluce Castle, followed by Dunseverick, and soon O'Neil had control of nearly every major city in Ireland. The peasant army was ferocious, and overtook the ill-prepared British occupants with relative ease, but O'Neil found that these peasants were unruly and would not conform to his commands. They began to massacre Protestant residents by the hundreds and though the Irish Catholics had secured control of the country, O'Neil and other nobles feared the anticipated backlash from Parliament.

British troops arrived shortly after the takeover, but soon left as Royalist and Parliamentarian civil wars were breaking out back home. O'Neil formed the Irish Catholic Confederations, and the island enjoyed independent rule for nearly seven years.

O'Neil was a hero to O'Rafferty and his household. O'Neil endowed O'Rafferty with land and a noble house on his land, and with O'Neil heavily involved in the political sphere on the island, O'Rafferty essentially ran the plantation. There was still some unrest on the island, but it was a time of relative peace. O'Rafferty stood tall each day, knowing he had stayed loyal to his friend, while also knowing that he didn't take part in the vile acts of the other peasant soldiers. He had stayed true in a life devoted to Christ and he did not succumb to the wickedness of murder. The O'Rafferty children were growing, and it was comforting to think that they could live in an independent country, something his father or his father's father could not say. He and Brigh were truly happy and they even allowed themselves to indulge in the past times of the town, such as going to the public house on Saturday evenings. While there, Brigh would sing and play her guitar while the other patrons sang and danced along. O'Neil would even stop in on occasion, along with some of the other heroes of the revolution. However, with all of this joy, there were still whispers from Britain of Parliamentary overthrow, the execution of Charles I, and the rise of Oliver Cromwell--a zealot bent on restoring the Protestant Church of England to all of the surrounding islands. Cromwell had reformed the British army into a professional unit, men devoted solely to life as soldiers. Cromwell was also incensed by O'Neil and the Irish Catholic Confederation's alignment with King Charles and the Royalists, and of course, the reports of the thousands of fellow Protestants being massacred on the Irish island.

With increasing panic that Cromwell and his forces would invade, James Butler, the Marques of Ormonde, gathered confederate and Royalist soldiers to take Dublin, and overthrow Michael Jones, the commander of the only Parliamentarian outpost in Ireland. With a successful siege of Dublin, Cromwell would have no friendly port to enter with his naval fleet, with Admiral William Penn and the like.

Ormonde gathered nearly eleven thousand soldiers, armed well with muskets and pikes supplied by the Papacy, and camped at the Dublin suburb of Rathmines. The army took hold of the Rathfarnham Castle in early August and Ormonde sent a regiment to then occupy Baggotrath Castle and thus closer to Dublin. However, this regiment was met by a garrison of Jones's troops already in Baggotrath Castle and were decimated by scores of musket blasts. The few surviving soldiers fled back to camp to warn Ormonde when they heard additional muskets firing and saw plumes of smoke blocking out the August sun. It was an ambush on all fronts. Thousands of confederate and Royalist troops were killed, and several were imprisoned, while the surviving troops returned to Ireland's walled towns, injured and low on supplies. Days later, Cromwell waltzed into Dublin undeterred, nearly thirty thousand professional soldiers strong.

Cromwell saw the easy landing on the island as a sign from God that his extermination of the Catholics in Ireland was providence. These Catholics had strayed from the path, and indulged in ornate structures and idolatry--putting their resources in cathedrals and monasteries while their people were poor and starving. Electing to pray to a saint or the Virgin Mary rather than shed themselves from their pugnacious, drunken ways. He would be the savior of these people. He would save them from themselves.

Cromwell marched on to the port city of Drogheda. The

Irish had a decent stronghold, as the city was walled and nearly three thousand soldiers were contained inside and archers manned the high towers. Cromwell knew Ormonde would resort to starving his, Cromwell's, army holding in their fortresses safely while Cromwell's men slowly ran out of resources. Cromwell could not be patient if his people were to live and the Catholics effaced. He assembled nearly six thousand soldiers led by Colonel Castle, his longtime friend, to storm the south walls and tower of Drogheda. It would be a bloody endeavor, but the taking of this port city meant further arms and delivery and future successful campaigns.

Arthur Aston, the Irish commander at Drogheda, hobbled with his forces to the city wall. Aston was a professional soldier who had fought against Parliament before, and was even held prisoner while fighting for Charles I at an outpost at Reading. He had known nothing but war, serving with his father since he could first recall, and yet lost his leg not from a bullet or bayonet, but from falling off his horse one day at the Oxford countryside. Rumors would swirl that within his wooden leg lay gold coins and jewels. His men despised him, but he instilled order and a killer's instinct in their hearts. They had, after all, taken up arms to defend their kinsmen and what was rightfully theirs. The British had shown them nothing but brutality, and it was brutality the British would receive in return. Aston knew the Irish supplies and manpower were depleted, but he also knew the British would be vulnerable if they were to attempt to breach any side of the citadel. He divided his troops to the four corners of the city and waited for the British to make their move. At noon, the west tower spotted a battering ram approaching with a regiment of soldiers. To Aston's surprise, a colonel was accompanying the troops. It was bad conduct to actively target an enemy's commanding officer, but Aston knew each action needed to be bold. Timidity would be death for this ancient yet fledgling nation. He also knew of Cromwell's zealotry and rigid belief in God's destiny for him. This type of man was very dangerous; a man whose righteousness deluged through his body and teemed out of his pores--a King

David or Jeremiah or Niallach or Charlemagne. In this man, the Earth was for the purge of the wicked in his mind into a purity of only those like minds or the willing to kowtow and stay silent. And, to this man, this iron-clad Roundhead commander and authority to all, death was but the will of God and a final act of everlasting redemption. Aston knew he was unlike his enemy, this Cromwell, for he feared death. He had witnessed kin and countrymen fall all of his life, and he was aware enough to understand that pain. That pain of wanting to die because of someone else's death. Aston had his wife and young son in this town. He was not a coward afraid to die. He was a lifelong soldier, but he thought of the morning as Lily would pour him a cup of ale and cook eggs and bacon and kiss him on the scar on his left cheek and hum softly to herself while she hurried Thomas to the breakfast table and they either sat and Aston made a quip and they all chuckled or they didn't say a word and Aston would watch the sparrows from the window leap into the sun and appear and disappear in the sun and James the shepherd would raise his staff for a hello to Aston as he and his flock shuffled past Aston's cottage window and man and flock climbed up the hillock until the fog wiped them clear from all vision. And so, Aston would be bold in his strategy and command archers to fire at the British colonel until his horse was spooked and veered away from the surrounding guard, the horse naying and lifting its front hooves off the ground and the British colonel flailing his sabre and yelling "The wall!" while Aston's soldiers flanked both sides of the invading forces and two dozen Irish soldiers fired at the colonel's head, piercing his chest and face and shooting his horse down too and the two dozen rushing forward and stabbing the colonel with their bayonets from all sides to such a degree that they could hear the ping of metal from one bayonet striking another while stabbing the colonel's torso.

The British forces, even with their colonel dead, continued to march against the Drogheda west tower. The Irish mowed them down in droves, but the British kept advancing and finally breached the wall, but could not push any farther as the bodies of their comrades impeded their progress and so retreated for the day.

Cromwell's resolve reached new heights once he heard of his slain friend, Colonel Castle. He amassed the full scope of his army and stormed the tower. Irish archers held their posts steadily, but the fatigue and lack of ammunition soon set in. Cromwell's voice echoed through the Drogheda streets. Mothers, children, and the infirmed began to flee to the other city towers and strongholds, if not fleeing the city with just the clothes on their backs altogether. O'Rafferty's sister Kathryn gathered her two boys and rushed towards Keegan, her husband, who came rushing down the street with a tourniquet on his right arm and a gash across his face. Other archers or pikemen followed behind and soon the sound of musket fire filled the air. Bodies fell all around the family, and the smoke from the rifles, as well as the ever encroaching cannons, engulfed the town. Keegan pushed Kathryn and his boys forward, shouting in a muddled Irish brogue, until he felt the musket ball pierce his thigh and he fell to his knees. Kathryn looked back, but he was soon gone in the smoke and a moment later dealt the death blow with a sabre across his neck. Aston and the remnants of his troops shot back blindly into the smoke and then retreated to the south tower which held their remaining munitions. Cromwell's cavalry cut through the smoke like apparitions of nightmare, their faces hidden from the gray and black clouds, and only the luster of the armor and blades could be seen. Aston hobbled along until two of his men swooped over and carried him to and inside the tower. As the smoke began to dissipate, and a handful of Irish rebels locked the tower doors and took up their arms, Cromwell and his horse stood, holding his rolled up decree for British Invasion and the terms of Irish surrender. Cromwell calmly read the decree with a wry smile in the corner of his mouth. It was all just bluster, the illusion of being a gentleman and civilized human. It was known by all in Drogheda that Cromwell meant punishment or death for these people, and when these people, who knew that surrender meant not death but life in bondage and without their faith, language, and land–knew it was better to die, and so as

Cromwell spoke his last words of armistice, Aston picked up a pike and threw it from the tower window down to Cromwell's feet. The British army heaved open the tower door as arrows rained down upon them. Irish pikemen swung valiantly, but the British simply stepped back, cocked their muskets, and obliterated rows of Aston's men until they finally conceded and Aston was wrangled down from the upstairs of the tower. Aston cursed and writhed as British soldiers carried him from all fours and threw him on the Drogheda ground. A soldier grabbed Aston's wooden leg and yanked it from his thigh. Soldiers banged the wooden leg against the cobbles of the street--the leg sounding hollow and containing no gold inside. With a small regiment of British soldiers surrounding and holding Aston down, he cursed and spat as they guffawed and mimicked his Gaelic curses as if they were spoken from a child. "Here ye, here ye, I knight you King of Ireland," one soldier said while using Aston's wooden leg as a ceremonial sword, tapping it from each of Aston's shoulders and then smacking him across the face with the wooden prosthetic. Each soldier took a turn bludgeoning Aston with his leg until Aston, bloodied from head to toe, lay nearly unconscious. The sea of soldiers surrounding Aston then parted and Cromwell came forward. They placed the leg in Cromwell's hands and he grinned, weighing the light peg. "You are truly worthless," he spoke and then lifted the leg into the sky and crashed it down onto the top of Aston's skull, cracking the weapon and its target in half.

Kathryn, her boys, and the other civilians were gathered by Cromwell's troops after they had finished their assault on the Irish rebels. Cromwell stood before the captured civilians, a crowd of nearly three thousand. They were pitiful and wretched and a stain on the British empire. How was God to place such tests before him? To create the corrupted, the testers of fortitude and will. Lesser leaders would bend before these creatures and compromise for peace. The true leader and pragmatist knew that peace was an illusion, a cheap parlor trick that only left the sucker empty handed. An idea of peace was a sign of weakness. A sign of mercy, after these now withered peasants were strong enough before to slaughter Protestants by the thousand, now begged for some reprieve. It would not happen. Cromwell could not allow another generation of Irish malcontents to slip through the cracks just to rise up again and lead to the demise of Cromwell and his kin. He had to be hard and decisive. They needed to know the consequences of rebellion.

Cromwell first called for the male children and lined them against the tower wall. Their mothers cried out and flailed their outstretched arms, for there was nothing else to be done. Cromwell's colonel ordered two rows of soldiers to raise their muskets with his sabre, and with a guttural "Fire" he swung the sabre down to his side and the boys fell like stalk on the scythe. A mother writhed to the ground and swung her fists at any soldier in her perimeter. Cromwell ordered her up and two soldiers escorted her to the mound of dead boys. She saw her son's red curly hair covered in blood with his eyes pressed shut as if willing the bullet away from his body and tragically knew that he had no will whatsoever, only to live to be some token of discipline for another type of holy war. She wailed to the sky with her dead son pressed against her chest. Mutters of horror filled the Drogheda street. The mother collapsed to the ground and laid like a sack of stones--wrecked and beyond any tears. Crowmwell's soldiers picked her up and placed her in front of the crowd of Irish peasants. With two rifles and the sun now clear, alone and beating down at the arrested image of two iron-clad veteran soldiers and one ragged, poor woman, two triggers were pulled and two metal balls left their chambers and exploded through the woman's skull and pungent, black-gray smoke entered the air. Somewhere past the walls of the town, finches flew indifferently in the same way they had done for thousands of years.

Cromwell had called for no quarter that day, and every unfortunate Irish soul on the grounds of Drogheda was massacred in a storm of metal, smoke, and fire. The few remaining rebel soldiers fled to the River Boyne, but were met by a squadron of British ships and blown away by cannon fire. A hundred other Irish soldiers hid in Saint Peter's Church until the building was set on fire and they were either burned or shot to death. After Cromwell moved to the next fortified Irish town, O'Rafferty made his way to Drogheda and identified Kathryn, his brother-in-law, and two nephews among the scores of dead bodies rotting in the streets. O'Neil was a fugitive of Cromwell's forces and had fled to an old crannog by Roughan Castle, and it was no longer safe for O'Rafferty's family on the plantation.

The O'Raffertys traversed the Irish forests to evade capture, and eventually settled in the Dun An Ri Forest. He and his family lived like beasts, scavenging for edible berries or leaves, and he would hunt with his bow and arrow. The songs were gone from Brigh's mouth, and she could no longer bring herself to read her Bible. She would simply sit by the brook and run her fingertips along the water and stare up at the cracks of sky through the trees. O'Rafferty thought about O'Neil often and wondered if a miracle had occurred and the Irish regained control of the island. He had pangs of regret about how he did not remain by his friend's side. He knew he was a coward who had put his family before his country. Now, he and Brigh and their four children walked the Earth like mice, scurrying away when an alien sound or a feint footstep in the distance was heard in the distance. They would most likely die of starvation in this forest anyhow; he may have well had died brave.

Inevitably, the day came when a regiment of Cromwell's soldiers combed through the forest and discovered the O'Raffertys. The family was sent to Dublin, where they were enslaved to the army to maintain food and munition supplies and unload cargo from British ships. He had mercifully been spared from execution, as his association with O'Neil and the Irish Confederation was not evident, but it was daily that a new head was delivered to the city of a revolutionary leader and placed on a spike in the center of town for all to see. One day, news came down that Felim O'Neil had finally been captured after a valiant defense at Charlemont, and was being taken to Dublin to receive his punishment. The trial was a mere formality when he arrived, as he was named the ringleader of the confederacy and convicted of high treason.

Before O'Neil's execution, O'Rafferty was granted visitation with him. O'Rafferty, seeing his friend bruised and chained, lowered his head in shame. "I should be in there with you," O'Rafferty finally whispered.

There was an immense silence, and then O'Neil said, "This is always how it would end for me. Keep your faith and your country with you and your family, and all of this will have been worth it. Just stay with me as long as you can. And tomorrow, do not witness the brutality they will bring upon me. Just go to the cathedral and say a Hail Mary for me."

The following day, O'Rafferty did as his friend had asked and entered Saint Patrick's Cathedral. Cromwell had repurposed the nave and the side aisle of the church as a horse stable, and the alter which once contained the Host was now occupied by crates of ammunition and hay, but the crucifix remained hanging from the ceiling. O'Rafferty genuflected, entered one of the few uncluttered pews, kneeled down, and began to pray with his rosary beads while in the center of the city his friend was being hanged, emasculated, disembowelled, beheaded, and chopped into four pieces to be spread across Ireland.

CHAPTER SIX

The mid-June afternoon sun baked on the sandstone steps of Father Judge as the eighth period bell sounded and the day was over, and over too was Connor Dempsey's time in high school. He walked down the staircase of the all-boys Catholic high school wearing his Columbia blue golf shirt uniform with the crucifix-embroidered emblem and the motto "Non Excidet" (He will not fail) bannered underneath and his charcoal gray slacks and GBX dress shoes with his black, empty Jansport backpack slung across one shoulder and his Master Lock, which he had used for four years, in his hand. Dempsey had his signature sideways grin upon his pale, freckled face, and his almost-white blonde curly hair began to sway slightly in the breeze. He crossed the street to Ramp Playground, opened his Master Lock, hooked it on the chain link fence by the basketball court, and closed the lock for the last time. Sheridan, Burke, and McNammara were already waiting by his Plymouth Reliant, and he walked toward his grandfather's car which was now his. Dempsey and his friends drove off with the summer and their lives ahead of them. He opened the window and let his hand glide with the wind as his music played along the neighborhood of Holmesburg in Philadelphia.

*

Thomas Holme climbed on his steady warhorse Magnus and fastened his short-barrel rifle to his hip and joined the rest of his dragoon unit march through the peat of Ireland. He recalled days walking over the steep hills and forest of Lancashire with his father, and then one day, when he was about six, his father simply not being there. His father had died suddenly while cultivating the eastside of his land, possibly by a fallen tree branch or a slip down into the valley, or some mysterious illness; maybe even foul play. Nonetheless, his father was but a vague image in his mind, with no distinct features, like viewing an acquaintance in a dream-- feeling his presence but not recognizing him. From there he was tasked with helping to raise his younger siblings until he was sent to Hawkshead Grammar School, where he learned his necessary writing acumen, but also his passion for illustrations. Holme thought of his last days there, brazenly carving his initials in a school desk and even depicting a live oak tree underneath. Now, he was part of the scourge of Ireland and Cromwell's bloodlust and the ultimate self-gratification that only one man is the divine mouthpiece of the Lord and all others must fall in line or else perish. Cromwell had once spoken out against such tyranny, but he was now, besides the actual crown on his head, the king of England. Holme thought of how easy it was for men to fall to the same corruption that they spoke out against. They derided the snake until they killed it, just to inherit its fangs the next day and pierce all others with its venom. Thomas Holme did not want to perform the acts required of him under Cromwell, but it was that, or perish himself. He had been a soldier since he was seventeen, and now at age twenty-seven and with a wife, Sarah, and child arriving, the guilt began to weigh on his soul. As a teenager, blood was a fine and necessary proposition. Rage and righteousness emanated in his body. He was ripe to accept hatred and act upon it. The Irish and any other rebellious lot were villains threatening to upheave and expunge English life. The rifle or sword felt right in his hand, and he fired or swung with a sense of duty and pride, and an easy simplicity. These actions would form a new way, a way without the chains of absolute rule and a life where only some could have the aspiration for freedom. He would fight valiantly and be rewarded with a world as it was meant to be lived, without the omniscient specter of government and religion, just a man who could wake, do as he pleased with the day, and be a kingdom within himself and his family.

As the years of fighting persisted, he knew this ideal world was not to be. He saw Parliament and the army fall into the same patterns of oppression. Citizens slaughtered without trial or reasons, soldiers committing the slightest infractions executed on the spot, and independent sects of Christianity, preaching tolerance and non-violence being jailed or shipped to English colonies. Holme did not have the answer to how life should be as he rode his horse towards Limerick with his fellow dragoons that day in this endless war, but he was certain that it had to be better than this.

CHAPTER SEVEN

Dempsey walked down the clearing of Pennypack Park and along the bike path that ran parallel to the creek. The water was only about knee deep, but plenty of people still swam in it. He was carrying his waders, tacklebox, and fishing rod, and on his way to meet Burke at the spot with the swinging rope by the small bridge. They had named the location Heaven, and it was the frequent spot for keg parties in the woods in high school and the soon to follow police raids. Those times were certainly fun, but it was lazy afternoons like this one that Dempsey cherished. He was anything but an adequate fisherman, but he enjoyed the prospect of just casting his line and seeing if anything would bite. He also liked the sensation of standing in the cool water in his waders watching the creek flow down over tiny stones with the sun reflecting above. Dempsey and Burke had a tradition of Saturday fishing in the creek for nearly two years, and though they both were staying in Philadelphia for college, Dempsey felt this would be one of the last times they would fish together. They had lived only two blocks from one another their whole lives, went to Saint Jerome's and Father Judge, played on Crispin baseball, and even had their first beer together, and now they would be apart. Burke was going to live in the dorms at Temple University, and dempsey would stay at home and go to community college for his associates and then study nursing, hopefully at Temple as well. It was more than a shared proximity that made them friends, at least to Dempsey. It was that first sense of brotherhood, that the world was not a hostile concept, but a place of discovery and fidelity.

Dempsey was seven and in the first grade at Saint Jerome's Elementary School. The school consisted of two identical three story buildings with a gap in between for a blacktop used for traffic and recess, and the church was situated in front of the two buildings with an adjacent parish green and rectory. The church contained a large oil painting on the altar of Saint Jerome, an elderly bald man with a long gray beard looking up and in the distance as if God was hovering above and ready to inspire his hand which held a quill next to the skull on his desk to write on the papyrus scroll in front of him either new words on the doctrine of the early Catholic Church or the translation of the scripture from Greek into Latin and which was to be known as the vulgate while a lion slept peacefully at his feet. Dempsey's mother drove him down Holme Avenue in the family Astrovan, he with his Spider-Man lunch box and matching school bag, baby blue collared uniform and his Coke-bottle glasses and curled blonde hair slicked and comber to the side with about a pound of L.A. Looks gel, staring out the window as they arrived to school for the first time. Dempsey looked out to see the other children walking with their mothers to the school entrance and then stopping as they reach the front steps to let out a fantastic cry and then run into their mother's arms sobbing and not wanting to let go. He feared he would do the same as he walked with his mother, but even after his mother gave him a kiss and told him she loved him, no tears came and he walked right into class. As he sat down in his seat in Miss Yonley's classroom, he realized that this would be it. There would be no more days where he could play with his action figures all day or lounge on the couch and watch Nickelodeon while at his Grandmother's house and wait for her to make vanilla popsicles or tell him all about her days of watching the Phillies at Connie Mack Stadium. He was now a big kid in school, and before he knew it, there was a notebook in front of him and he had to trace upper and lower case "A".

After writing, they gathered in a circle on the rug and Miss Yonley read them a Dr. Seuss book. Dempsey could not help but drift off and start looking at the girl who sat across from him. She had golden pigtails, radiant green eyes, and the sweetest smile. Without realizing it, he had been staring at this girl, Lauren, and she soon enough raised her hand and told the teacher "Connor is looking at me" and he quickly drew his eyes to the ground.

After snack time, Dempsey went with the other boys to the bathroom. The urinals reached the floor, and Dempsey feared that he would urinate on his new dress shoes. After that fear subsided, he washed his hands and ran with the other boys down the hallway. Nearly to Miss Yonley's room, a short, old, black-haired woman emerged from the corridor and stopped him. Her skin was dry, wrinkled, and a shade of umber, and she wore thick, yellow-tinted octagonal shaped glasses, and she had on a gray blazer and matching skirt. Her lips pursed back and forth between snarl and grimace, and her nostrils flared and exhaled heavily.

"Don't you know you can't run in the hallway!" she spoke in a venomous twinge. "You could hurt yourself or others. I should call your mother!"

Dempsey stood, trembling and unable to produce a sound,

"Get to class and don't let me catch you running again!"

When it was finally time for lunch, Dempsey sat beside a brown-haired boy eating a peanut butter and jelly sandwich and a Capri-Sun.

"That was Sister Fiscetti that yelled at you," the boy said while smacking his peanut butter filled lips. "She is the meanest person in the world. My two brothers would always get in trouble with her. My one brother gave her the finger one time. They're a lot older than me."

"What's the finger?"

"I don't know. It's bad though. My name is Vince."

"I'm Connor. Want to be friends?"

"Sure."

Dempsey sat by the edge of the creek, daydreaming into the Pennypack water until Burke arrived. Burke had grown his hair to the nearest centimeter of acceptability at Judge, and now, since graduating, he was content to keep growing it for the foreseeable future. His hair would one day match his idols from classic rock-- Mick Jagger, Jimmy Page, Jim Morrison, and so on. HE even wore aviators and sported sideburns and wore jeans whenever he could.

Burke had also picked up the habit of smoking cigarettes, which seemed to match his whole get-up.

The two donned their waders and marched into the creek. Burke was really no better a fisherman than Demspey, but he would always say he had learned a new technique from his father. Burke's father was in the local steamfitters union, and he was an omnipresent figure in Burke's life. From little league games for Crispin to buying the occasional case of beer for Burke and winking at him and telling him not to tell his mother, his father was always there, and Burke idealizing him in return. Burke would always have a new tale to tell of his father's days in the neighborhood in the seventies, drinking and causing hell, fighting for fun or honor and just good old no good mischief. However, through Burke's compulsory need to top his father's antics, there was a vibrant spirit and intelligence. Although he would not admit it, it was not too long ago that Burke was winning math competitions and read-a-thons at Saint Jerome's and receiving a scholarship to Father Judge and being ranked in the top twenty of the school in GPA until drinking took more of a priority in his life and he slipped to 45 at the time of graduation. Even so, Burke was better than them all, and it often baffled Dempsey that he would squander such gifts. Maybe Burke would figure it out in time, and let them all have it.

They cast out their lines and stood in the creek waiting for a bite. After a while, they could both see large catfish wriggling past their feet. The fish got as close to the hooks to sniff the bait, a compound they purchased at Linden's Tackle Shop, but they just as soon swam away.

"They won't eat it. They never will," Burke concluded.

"They're after something else," Dempsey responded.

"Or they've felt the hook before, and they don't want to feel it again."

*

Sarah returned from Tewkesbury with her newborn son in her arms. He was named Thomas after his father, and the three would live in Limerick as Thomas Senior oversaw repairing

Core Castle. Pockets of rebellion still existed in these days, with a surprise bloody encounter still springing up, usually when it seemed that the island had finally reached a peace. Irish rebels would breach a castle wall at night or ambush a reconstruction unit and Sarah would have to place young Thomas in the care of her maid and begin dressing wounds or plying soldiers with whiskey until their shrieks of pain subsided. This all needed to end at some point, but it never would. She at least admired Thomas's drive to forge his own path. While other soldiers complained about late or missing wages, Thomas remained diligent and reserved, choosing each word wisely and taking any opportunity that came his way. Thomas served under Colonel Sands, a zealot's zealot who would almost put Cromwell to shame. Sands would rant and rave about the plague of the Irish loud and unbridled so anyone in the closest decimated town could hear, and most likely just stirred further rebel outbreaks. Sands was mad and treated his men even worse, but he was a skilled surveyor and visionary--seeing this land of rubble as a fresh pallet for him to create his masterpiece, the groundwork of a British Protestant utopia under the rule of a collective body fronted by a strong, charismatic yet pious leader, Cromwell, who would wipe the Catholic idolatry and decadence away and create a state of living devoted to one another in a collective sharing of masteries for one united purpose, to serve in Christ.

As cantankerous as Sands seemed to be, his passion was at least laudable. He had construction always on his mind, with this love of building going beyond the stone and cement and T-squares of the earth, but of what could be built in man. How he cherished seeing a bold, defiant young soldier fall into line after witnessing Sands's rough justice to insubordination, to that soldier then evolving from the mindless grunt and musket fodder to want to take part in this better version of the world. This soldier who realized that war was useless if it did not spur progress, for it always did. Beyond the death, it was competition, it was sport--testing one's will against another man's in the toughest of conditions, leaving that conscious, self-perseverance to think only of fighting so the man beside you does not die, and if that man does not die, then your country does not die, and the dream with it.

As Thomas worked with Sands from sun-up and sun-down, Sarah would bathe young Thomas, walk the streets of Limerick, and even forged friendships with some of the locals. Soon, she grew fond of the island, but resented the still ever-present threat of warfare. The British government was certainly not as fair and righteous as it believed itself to be. Enforcing law and justice would never change, but she despised how her Lord was so strictly defined. It ran counter to the words of Christ she read in the gospel. To her, it just reeked of the lust for power in men. Not only was it essential for men to establish dominion of the earth and one another, they also had to control their destination in the afterlife. So, when a charismatic young preacher entered Limerick, she was prepared to listen, as he spoke her heart.

His name was George Fox, and he spoke not of doctrine and penalties for disobedience, but simply of religion as a gathering of friends, treating each other with kindness and putting another's needs before your own. He did not finish his speech with a caveat, asking for a donation for the church and so on, but he simply told of their meeting place, a nondescript hall at the edge of town.

She told Thomas of this speaker, and the two soon attended a meeting. The two were swept away by this speaker and his gathering of friends. Fox did not speak of decoration or sacrament or eternal salvation or anything of that kind; he just talked of tolerance, something that seemed desperately needed in a time of bloodshed and grief.

This group of friends continued to grow and soon fell under the scrutiny of the Protestant government. Members were placed in jail or exiled to islands such as Barbados, but the resolve of the group did not waver. How could it, for they only spoke of peace. Eventually, they came upon the name Quakers, and Sarah and Thomas were soon good friends with the former British admiral's son, William Penn.

CHAPTER EIGHT

Michael Dempsey, Connor's father, sat in his recliner on a Friday night and watched the Phillies' game. His feet were sore from a busy, hot day of landscaping for Mercer Lawn Care , where he coordinated the routes for the mowers and treatment sprayers, and worked personally on high-end projects for the wealthier clients in areas such as Yardley. He changed careers a few times in his life, but he had been with Mercer for nearly fifteen years now. Al Mercer, the owner, treated him fairly well, and Michael was essentially the second in command, and practically ran the business, as Al could be flighty and vanish for sometimes weeks at a time. When Al was around they were good friends and would often go out to a bar, such as Ashton Tavern, after work. The work itself had become less physically demanding as he progressed through the company, but there would still come a time when he had to carry large stones or slabs of granite while working on a project, and he would have to sub and mow a lawn if a worker did not show up. He had kept the family well afloat with this job, but he would have moments of intense bitterness and regret that he couldn't provide more for his family, especially when working on an expensive home or mansion in the suburbs. Here he was, at age fifty, still stuck in a Philadelphia row home, practically in the same neighborhood his entire life. His wife, Tara, and son, Connor, never even said a word when it was apparent that the family could not afford to send Connor to a college like Temple or La Salle, at least for a few years, while all of his friends were preparing to live in the dorms in one of the city colleges or Penn State or another Pennsylvania school. His younger sons, Kevin and John, also adapted well and never whined or pouted when the didn't get what they wanted. The family was tough and thankful for what they had, but Michael believed it should have been different. He did not have the chance to go to college and become a CPA or something along those lines. He was a musician and painter in high school, and had the crazy dream that he could make it with his art. However, the Vietnam War happened and he was drafted. He went from playing guitar and singing with his buddies or painting a landscape on the weekend, to a buzz cut and five AM trainings and firing a rifle while on his stomach or crawling through the mud underneath barbed wire. He had fortunately seen little action while serving in the army, but it was still those sensations stuck in his memories that got to him. Receiving the draft letter and report date of June 6th, driving around Mayfair in his father's car with no destination, just mindlessly turning the wheel and stepping on the pedals and studying each street sign and becoming angry that he had not known them all by heart, or passing a storefront that he had not seen before and wondering how long it had been there and how lucky the people inside were that they were not drafted and awaited either death or four years as a young man taken away to fight for some cause that you don't even quite understand, and those people in that store had their whole lives to walk that same streets and know each road like an old friend, then he would snap out of it and think about his own father and fighting in Japan and coming back to Philadelphia and buying property to be built on this field land outside of Center City and being surrounded on that row home by other G.I. World War II veterans and being there for one another and having children at the same time and the children playing with one another and then suddenly happy that he went through such hardship because now the world was a free place and oppression would be effaced and the slate wiped clean and then they had you duck under your desk at school and prepare you for an atom bomb dropped on your head and then you see Elvis and the Beatles on television and you start to play the guitar and you can remember the pain of first pressing your fingers against the strings and then you learned your first chord and then you made your first riff and you played with your buddies AJ, Dave, and Skip and you at least figured out how to sing and play the guitar at the same time and although you sounded like Bob Dylan or a nasally folk singer you became the lead and played with your band in Dave's garage before his pop came home from the night shift at the Nabisco factory and your father beat you with his belt when you failed Algebra for the semester and you just stood there and took it even though you were about his size and much more spry but he had seen war and he was your father and the sting of his belt made you want to cry but you weren't a pussy so you didn't and you wore a shirt and tie and blazer to Father Judge every day and rode the bench on the football team and took Art because it was an easy A as you told your buddies but you secretly loved it and scribbled a few trees in a forest but you hated that you didn't try harder because you could have done better and then one day you heard seniors talking about joining the army and fuckin' up the Commies and you frothed at the mouth like they had but then you thought of yourself holding a rifle or killing a man and being killed and you just wanted to leave the building and have a cigarette in Pennypack Park because your father forbade smoking and had his mail route down the street and would give you the belt if he saw a Pall Mall in your mouth and then you heard one day Billy McGovern had died over in Vietnam and Father Judge held a mass in the gymnasium and they had that photo of Billy in his Marines' uniform and hair buzzed so straight that you could balance a tennis ball on it and the wreath with the semper Fi banner across the middle and the altar boys processed up the aisle in their white cloaks and black bibs holding candles with plastic drip guards and another altar boy carrying a large golden rod with a crucifix on top and the class president, Pat Conley, carrying the sword of the crusader, the school mascot, and the vice president behind him carrying the scabbard and then Father Morley in his satin robes and his white collar sticking out of the top and you realized the day would come when you would be upon that stage accepting your diploma and you could be on the stage once again with your goofy grin and military cut with your guts splattered somewhere you've never

MATTHEW GLASGOW

heard of before and then Father Morley expounds on how brave you were and how much you loved your country and that you were now in heaven with Jesus and your spirit would be looking over everyone and your mother would sit at the dining room table going through the mysteries of her rosary and go to church and place a quarter in the donation box and light a candle for your memory.

Michael gazed at the television screen blankly and sipped his beer which only made him drowsy these days. Habit after habit, erasing thought and feeling with routine. The game concluded and Michael looked at the clock, which read ten P.M., and then began to fall asleep. His wife, Tara, a nurse, was working all night at Frankford-Torresdale Hospital, Kevin and John were on their Playstation in their room, and Connor was out with friends, so he just rolled on his side while on his recliner and slept as the television remained on.

At about two thirty in the morning, he heard the back door slam open and went to the stairs. Connor was staggering through the dark attempting to find the staircase. He was drunk to the point of incoherence.

"Dad. Why are you awake? I was with Burke and all them," Connor garbled out with his eyes barely open.

"Couldn't sleep I guess," he said and guided his son to the staircase.

Connor talked in a slurred babble and reeked of cheap booze, most likely malt liquor. He placed him on the couch, and Connor was immediately asleep.

He had never envisioned that he would be a father. After four years in the army he returned home to his parents. His father was diagnosed with lung cancer less than a year later, and it seemed like another three years of nothing but hospital trips, odd labor jobs, and going to the bar in between. He didn't have a problem with booze in those days, it was just what you did, and he did it nearly nightly, just like Connor seemed to be doing now in his summer before college. Seeing his father so infirmed sure didn't help matters either. His father was a hard-nosed asshole,

49

but he was always strong. He preached hard work and backed it up every day. That drive certainly led to his anger issues and smoking like a locomotive, but he had done it for his family. Every bag of mail he lugged in the cold sleet and snow was to put bread on that table and now he was a frail, bruised and yellow old man with a polka-dot hospital gown on and tubes and wires coming out of every which way. His father lied in that bed and hated it, not because he was sick, but he hated being inactive. He hated people making a fuss over him. He hated people looking at him waiting to die, which he did one January morning. Michael then stayed at home to take care of his mother and find his career. Then one Saturday night he went out with his buddy to Ashton Tavern and he drew up the courage to talk to this pretty blonde from across the bar.

Tara liked him from the start, though she was coming off a bad breakup and didn't want to place herself in a position of vulnerability quite yet. She had gone to Father Judge's sister, all-girls' school, Saint Hubert's, and she had heard his name through friends of friends, and she always thought he was kind of cute. He had dirty brown hair that curled around his ears, and pale blue eyes the color of a frozen lake. She knew he had been drafted for Vietnam as well, and her mind wandered in whether or not he saw any action or killed anybody and if it was as hellish as it seemed in the news and movies. Her own father had been in World War II and then moved the family to the Northeast when he returned, and he never once talked about it.

It was rare for her to be in a bar since she barely drank, but her friends kept pushing and prodding and telling her to "put herself out there" and she finally relinquishing and here she was talking to Michael Dempsey, nodding and trying to look pretty and thinking of something interesting to say next. All she could seem to think about was her patient from her night shift at Frankford-Torresdale, an old man clutching his stomach and writhing on the bed and yanking his catheter out and trying to grab her ass as she reached over to tuck his blanket in and then she storming out of the front doors and wondering "Is this what you get for helping people? Old perverts trying to fondle you and your boyfriend out at a bar cheating on you with some barely eighteen-year-old with a fake I.D."

Michael was patient with her and did not try to sweet talk her. They talked about Grandfunk Railroad and *Taxi* and took a shot of Old Grandad together after being dared by Sully the barfly and both gagged and coughed after taking it and she kissed him on the cheek at closing time, and even though he was starting to get drunk, he did not get aggressive with her and they made a date to go to lunch the next day at The Dining Car for some French Onion Soup.

Five years later they were married at Saint Bartholomew's and had their reception at the Knights of Columbus. They weren't sure about kids but that summer as newlyweds they went to Ocean City and saw all of the boys and girls running down the boardwalk and playing on the beach and riding the roller coasters that they began to try and the following April Connor was born.

When they first held their newborn boy, they knew they had made the right decision. Tara had a renewed zest for why it was so important to care for another. There were the helpless and the sick and diseased that needed tenderness, that needed a soft hand or voice to guide them through their pain. Connor, so little in her arms, was that pureness, that innocence, that blank page that needed to be filled with words that were right and kind and beautiful and true.

So she worked only the night shift so she wouldn't miss her days with Connor, even if it meant virtually no sleep and Michael bounced between labor jobs before landing with Mercer Lawn Care and soon she was pregnant once again with Kevin and then two years after that with John. Connor was always curious and willing to learn with an exuberance that rippled through the family. He would run up and down the steps playing Spider-Man or Batman or Ninja Turtles and Tara even made him a red bandana so he could be Raphael. She would read to him every night before bed and taught him the alphabet and his numbers. When he began to read, she noticed him squinting and struggling immensely at reading the words, so he took a vision test and needed strong prescription glasses. Connor never complained once and resumed bounding through the house in his large glasses that blurred his beautiful eyes and he wore Rec Specs when playing sports. Michael coached his little league team and would have a catch with him in the driveway nearly nightly. It irritated Michael that they couldn't practice grounders on a nice lawn in the backyard, but they made due. They would go to the baseball fields at Pollock Playground or Crispin or Thomas Holme and play for hours, and when they were old enough, Kevin and John would come too. Connor became a decent hitter and fielder, and even pitched on occasion as he progressed through Crispin Athletic Club, and he would wear that Crispin "C" hat, which was really just a Chicago Cubs hat, everywhere he went, except school of course, where he was forced to wear his dorky, gelled comb-over until kids started to biff their hair in the fifth grade. How quick it really does go, Michael thought as he put a blanket over Connor, who was passed out on the couch. He's already done high school, off to college, drinking with buddies in the woods, and he'll be working and have a family before I know it too. Michael walked up the stairs and slipped into his empty bed as Tara walked the hospital floor, feeling the dull pain in her back and wishing for the night to end.

CHAPTER NINE

He had one image, one tableau in his mind as he and his advisors and confidants sailed back from Hispaniola: it was the golden crown and scepter gently laying on the uncut purple velvet table, members of Parliament gathered around in the great hall in their long, curled wigs and colonels and generals of his New Model Army with polished silver breastplates and scabbards, all men with giddy smiles on their visages, all looking at him, Oliver Cromwell, the man who had taken down a tyrant and quenched revolutions in Ireland and Scotland, and had brought Mother England into a time of relative peace and a global juggernaut, growing colonies in the Caribbean islands and the new world of America, and more importantly and justly, brought God, the real God, back to his people. All of them waiting for this great man to be thus greater and humbly kneel down on one knee and them to place the crown on his head and place the fine fur on his shoulder and place the scepter in his hand and allow them to call him king. He knew that this offer was of the utmost genuine of sentiments, as every man in the room despised kings and monarchy as much or greater than Cromwell himself, and that they presented the crown to him because they truly believed in him and knew he was not their leader because of royal blood and providence, but that he placed each English man before himself for love of country and religion, and he had been the pragmatic yet brave man who was worthy to lead. He was their king because he did not desire to be their king, and perhaps because they knew that he would do exactly as he had done, deny the crown and say he would only be their protector and not their ruler.

They had taken his words to heart and named him Lord

Protector of England. He had fought against ceremony or any royal semblance, but they had convinced him it was for the good of England, that the people needed to see their leader as clearly not an ordinary man. They needed the formality, to see the rich garbs and glittering symbols. So they had him walk down the aisle and sit in King Edward's chair and they put the tapestries on his shoulders and they placed the scepter in his hands and they all bowed to him and the trumpets blared and he looked into the crowd and knew that no matter the title he was their king, and even he could not stop this worship of men. He sat on the king's chair and thought of his days as a young man in fury for the dissolute rule of King Charles and pounding his fist on the table and calling for justice and a government that speaks for the people and then the uprise actually happening and Charles tried and beheaded and soon Cromwell was in Ireland and killing those who were now leading a revolution against him and he figured his day would most likely come as well but maybe he could move the needle of man just enough that things would change and whether he be loved or hated, the hearts of man could live in bravery and in service of something greater than themselves.

The sea was turning his stomach and he began to sweat from his brow. He sat down on a bench on the starboard side and dreamily looked at the waves dancing endlessly, one action influencing the next in an eternal back and forth, ultimately meaning nothing. He scratched at the mosquito bites on his arms. He had fought in countless battles and no man had ever drew his blood, but this lowly insect had the gaul to land on his skin and draw its greedy beak into his, the Lord Protector of England's, body. He stared deeper into the waves and began to see snakes underneath the waves. These snakes, black, blue, and green, were soon the waves themselves, myriad for as far as he could see. They hissed and lashed their tongues at him and then began to cry, death wails, sounding like humans begging for mercy. Their reptilian faces morphed into faces of pale men and women and then the snakes became arms and hands reaching out to him and then he saw Achan of ancient Israel squirming out of the crowd with golden cups and jewels and then surrounding Achan were all of the spoils of Jericho and then the ocean turned to blood and the spoils were washed away and the hands returned holding stones and the stones were hurled at Achan until he lay prostrate on the sea of hands and the stones buried his lifeless body and the hands grew long and tentacled and built great castles with the stones while other hands pulled the stones apart and crumbled the castles and sprigs of clover emerged from the stone and then he saw his little daughter, Elizabeth, frolicking in the clover with her curly hair bouncing on her shoulders and then she began to rapidly grow and age until she was a woman and looked at Cromwell with her ice-blue eyes and held his sword covered in blood and she floated to the gunwale of the ship and tapped his shoulders with the bloody sword until it was the shape of a crown and placed it on his head and told him this is what you deserve and then she grew pale and emaciated and then her skin was nearly translucent and her eyes rolled to the back of her head and her cheeks caved into themselves and her lips shriveled into the back of her skull and she dissolved into a pillar of sand and then blew away and he fell to the floor of the ship.

The ship reached England and his colonels carried him down and into his room where he raved like a mad man for days until finally, after and lifetime of fighting, he slipped into death. His body was draped in kingly robes and the scepter and crown were placed in his tomb, and it was not for a year after his burial that his body finally felt the conclusion it knew it would and it was hanged outside of Westminster Abbey for a day, and then it was decapitated and the Cromwell head jammed on top of a twenty foot spike until a storm broke the pole in half and the head rolled away with the rain.

***

Penn and Holme, with his teenage son Thomas walked along the fields of Limerick. Sarah had passed the autumn before, and Holme was still adjusting to his added parental role in the household. Sarah and Thomas had lived together in Limerick for nearly twenty years, Sarah giving birth to ten children, with six passing away within the year. Sarah seemed to work every minute of her life, nursing wounded soldiers, taking care of the children, and cooking and cleaning the house. Then, becoming a prominent force in the Children of Light, the Society of Friends in Ireland, and even getting arrested on several occasions. So it was truly unfair for her to be stricken with a fever one evening, and not able to leave her bed for a week and die in a cold sweat while Thomas held her hand and the children gathered around her bed. There now, with Sarah gone and his religion as a Quaker facing heavy persecution from the government, seemed to be very little left for him in the United Kingdom.

"Following Father's death, King Charles has granted me the territory of West Jersey. My father served the crown well and this is what he has been gifted," Penn spoke while tucking a strand of hair behind his cap. He had smallpox as a child and had to wear a wig until he was eighteen. He now took pride in having his own hair and took great care in making sure it was presentable.

Thomas nodded solemnly and waited for Penn to continue, as Holme often contemplated deeply before responding.

"Our kind are no longer wanted here. We have faced great abuses and imprisonment. Our eyes have witnessed only blood on these lands. Kings live long enough just to be hanged and have their guts spilled across the island. We can create our own path. We can learn from their errs. It's a new world. A new life."

"I have property here, Penn. I've worked hard to gain the status I now have."

"But how many times have they taken what's yours? How many times will they do it again? You are a noble, but you are still under the yoke of the crown, and whatever their current whims may be."

"You speak truth. What would be my role?"

"I want a great city in this new land. My cousin, Silas Crispin, unfortunately passed on his way to, well, Charles commissioned the land to be called Pennsylvania."

"Ha. Your humility astounds."

"If anything, it is for Father's memory."

Penn thought of his father often. He remembered the summer when his father left for Ireland, and he did not return for over a year. He remembered their neighbor, Samuel, drunkenly staggering into the family parlor and reaching for his mother's breasts and then, when she shoved him away, making his way over to his sister to try to do the same. Penn remembered his father marching down the road and beating Samuel to a bloody pulp and then taking his sword out to finish the deed, but then lowering it and placing it back into his holster. It was this rage that often returned when he thought of his father, Admiral William Penn. Penn recalled coming back from school at age eighteen and raving about this Society of Friends who preached peace, and his father caning him until he was out onto the road and sent to Paris to get away from these "Friends" the following day. Penn did not relent, keeping his pen and voice active so all could experience this Society of Friends and become Children of Light. He was jailed many times and even thrown into the Tower of england and deprived food and water and threatened with life imprisonment, but he did not budge. This world of bloodiness and death needed to stop, and if he be the sacrifice so life wasn't a series of deaths at the mercy of some crazed tyrant, than so be it. His father would intervene and place his bail, though Penn did not want it, and his father would snarl and reprimand Penn for his dissonance and stubbornness and backwards religion, with Penn's only response being "I can only do what is in my heart; what I feel is right" until his father grew old and sick and smiled on his son and said that "I now understand. Even if I disagree, you are only doing what i have done my entire life. You are braver than I could have been with the blade" and he passed one cool September night in 1670.

"I would like you to be my surveyor for these new lands. To help to forge the great city of the world. A city of brothers and sisters. A place of no malice and avarice. You see it here in the hills of Ireland. These people crave peace. A new world, a blank slate, a new Eden under the providence of God. Are you my man for this?"

Holme saw these lands and he saw Sarah. She was in the shorelines and in the public houses and cobblestone roads. She was in each leaf of each clover, each cloud along the cliff. It would be the challenge of his life, but the time of serving just to have the bread ripped from your mouth was over. It was time to go.

"Yes. I am your man."

"I knew you would be. We sail on the Amity in April under Captain Richard Diamond. Make your arrangements and prepare your provisions. It is at least a two-month's journey, and the seas are rough, but the seas of change always are."

CHAPTER TEN

It was Thanksgiving morning, and Dempsey, Burke, McNamara, and Sheridans sat under the Pollock Playground "A" and each drank a 40 of Colt 45. The four had been up all night drinking in Burke's parents' garage, finally all reunited after nearly a semester away at college, all that is, except Dempsey who was very much still living in Holmesburg with his parents and attending community college. Burke's hair was nearly down to his shoulders, and he spent the evening talking about wild parties on Diamond Street, dodging the Temple Police on many occasions, and getting into a few spats right on Liacouras Walk. McNamara, who also attended Temple, would chime in when Burke was out of breath, and he too now smoked cigarettes. McNamara played baseball and basketball at Father Judge, and was for the most part a stiff when it came to partying, but with a few months with Burke, he was soon coming out of his shell. He was quiet, but loyal, and never had a bad thing to say about anyone in the group. Sheridan, a lanky brunette with a close-cropped haircut, was studying to be a pharmacist at Penn. His intelligence astounded them all and perhaps more astounding was that he chose to hang around them. His interests were always fleeting, as it would appear he would master one thing, get bored, and then move on to something else. He had played guitar and played a flawless "Stairway to Heaven", and then seemed to never play again. He did Jiu-Jitsu, choked out Domms, the toughest kid at Judge, and then stopped that too. He seemed to be into Martin Scorsese films now, and talked incessantly about the film's score and use of rock music to illustrate deeper themes.

After a night of drinking, they had all been feeling fairly

inebriated. It was a liberating thing in a way, drinking in the early morning at Pollock, under the concrete pavilion with its two triangular arches that resembled the letter A. They drank here in high school, but the fear was missing curfew or punishment by parents for drinking. Now they were college students and they felt untouchable. Still discreet enough, but knowing they were adults, though the drinking age dictated otherwise. "If I can die for my country, I can drink," Burke would often repeat. Everyone would snicker at this comment, but they all believed it as well.

It was a quarter after six, and the sun was beginning to come up. It was cold, but Dempsey felt good. Even though he had been up all night, he felt good. No, that was no way to describe it, but the alcohol pushed out most of his cognisance, and he was fully in the wonderful moment, when there was no antagonism or rush of anger or intense love, just being present with his three friends on a great holiday devoted to food, drinking, football, and thanks. It was fairly trite, but he was at least thankful to have such a moment back. He had feared they would leave him behind; latch on to friends at college, be enwrapped in some type of political activism, or, heaven-forbid, join a fraternity. They had remained relatively the same, and Dempsey was pleased. School at community college had hardly been much of a departure from high school, and he still felt like an adolescent since he lived at home, like he overslept graduation and when he woke up, everyone was gone and he was stuck at home in Holmesburg.

Sheridan began to climb up the nearly vertical slope of the Pollock A. It was made of a hardy concrete and had layers of wax and grease, whatever the parks people could do to prevent kids from climbing to the top. Sheridan wiggled and gripped carefully, and with a lovely drunken abandon, pumped and pushed his way forward until he had reached the summit. The crew hooted and hollered as he made the fantastic feat, and looked up at him in admiration. His athleticism seemed to know no bounds.

"Come on up and live a little," Sheridan bellowed, "You need to check out this view."

Pollock Playground was built on the peak of a hill

sandwiched between Welsh and Ashton Roads, so looking out, you were nearly eye-level with the tops of the trees of Pennypack Park. Below the A was the recess area for Pollock Elementary, with the three story school building at the perimeter. Standing tall on the building was the school's smoke stack, which had an ever-flashing red light at its top.

The sun was beginning to peek out from behind the trees, and the cool breeze felt fine.

"You stay up there, Sheridan, and we'll head to the bridge," Burke retorted and began to walk away. "Thanks for the 40 too."

Burke walked all the way to the playground exit, paused for effect, and then turned around and sprinted for the A. In a flash, he was up.

Dempsey and McNamara passed the 40s up and then climbed the A as well. He had been at the A more times than he could remember, but he never dared to climb it, like some of the old "Pollock Heads" or members of "PLK". It was fairly inane, but he was finally up, and sarcastic as Sheridan may have been, he was right. The view was fantastic. He could almost see it all-- Cars driving by on Ashton Road, an old man walking his labrador, the desolate property known as Farmer's, Winchester Swim Club, Holme Circle, and 7-11. The sunrise could have made him weep. Still feeling the buzz from the alcohol, his skin began to tingle and he lost himself in the fading blacks, grayish blues, and burning orange of the new day. It was all perfect and good in this moment.

"You ever hear the story of the kid in the smokestack?" McNamara interrupted the serense moment. "He climbed that thing on top of Pollock and fell in. They couldn't find him for weeks, until the smell started to travel across the whole neighborhood."

"Shit," Burke commented and sipped his 40.

At eight, the four descended from the A, walked across the Pollock baseball fields, and onto the railroad tracks. The tracks reminded Dempsey of many carefree afternoons, walking with Sheridan, Burke, McNamara, or some of their early elementary school or high school friends on their way to the Bluegrass Mall to get new CDs at Tower Records or to get lunch at Taco Bell or the Pizza Buffet. They would head home, bellies bloated, each vowing to burn copies of their new CD for one another, and they would then head Burke's or Sheridan's to play Grand Theft Auto or some football in the backyard. Standing on the tracks also brought vivid snips of memory--Dom Watts chucking pebbles at pigeons nesting at the underpass, nicking one to the point that it fell prone on the gray and cobalt blue stones between the railroad planks, and Watts finding a brick and a mere moment before ending the maimed creature's life when Dempsey intervened and simply told him it was wrong; the crazy biker kid who rode as fast as he could down Ashton Road as the freighter train rolled by and braking inches away from impact, the brakes reverberating through the neighborhood; the girl who showed her breasts on the track to a group of boys for a measly fifteen dollars. It all flooded back as he walked along with his friends toward the Holme Avenue Bridge in Pennypack, where Tom Palladus was having a Pre-Turkey Bowl Keg Party.

They passed Farmer's house, which was about five acres of land with a tiny, dark house, and four rusted out Chevy trucks. When they were in about eighth grade, local boys would sneak on Farmer's property. Some said they saw Farmer and he was an old black man who wore a black stetson hat, which kids compared to Freddy Kreuger. One story that circulated in the neighborhood was that a group of boys, troublemakers, a year older than Dempsey, egged Farmer's house one night and were subsequently stalked for the rest of the night by the old man in his old Chevy. The boys darted through Winchester Swim Club, and Farmer was there. They scurried down Ax Factory Road, and Farmer was there at the dead end in his old truck. They ran into the woods and swore they heard him following, and sprinted all the way down Solly Avenue, where the Pennypack trail was bisected. The idea that Farmer was some type of boogey man made Dempsey laugh to himself, but there was this level of mystery in the solitary man living on this large but dilapidated stretch of land that sparked his curiosity. He imagined this man living in the peaceful, undeveloped countryside outside of central Philadelphia, and then suddenly all of these contractors and real estate moguls coming in and buying up every square inch around him bulldozing trees, laying down asphalt and sidewalks, and building street after street of row homes while he just sat on the porch of his simple farmhouse observing it all, and probably thinking it has all gone to shit, as scores of white G.I.s with their uniform haircuts and three to five kids took over and never even cared to learn his name and just said he was the farmer and their bratty grandkids now comparing him to a horror villain and egging his house for fun.

The four continued on the tracks until they reached the Holme Avenue Bridge and to Palladus's keg party underneath. It seemed as if everyone Dempsey had ever known was at the party--from his Judge classmates to girls from Saint Hubert's and Basil's, most girls with blue and red stripes on their face for Judge. Dempsey's old girlfriend Ashley was there as well, and she looked even prettier than he remembered. They had dated junior and senior year until she broke his heart and ended it in May. She was going to Shippensburg for college, and she probably assumed he was just going to be a loser who lived at home and would never leave the Northeast. Her prediction was accurate so far, but it would not be for long. Dempsey would be in nursing school and living downtown with Burke and McNamara and having parties and inviting classmates from Temple and she would be wrong about him, so wrong, and he would be making more money than she with her Psychology degree, and he would have a beautiful wife and kids in a big house in the suburbs. Still, that was all so far away, and right now, sipping his plastic cup of Natural Light was just about all that he needed and then Palladus pulled out a bottle of vodka and he took a swig and passed it to Towers, who went to Penn State, and Towers scoffed at the bottle, which had about four ounces of vodka remaining and chugged it all down and let out an authoritative gasp and then a moment later threw it all up and then the party made their way to Lincoln's stadium for the game and no one even went inside to watch the game but just continued to drink in the parking lot and Dempsey saw even more people and then stumbled home and passed out on the couch and slept right through Thanksgiving dinner.

***

Holme had sailed on the ocean for an eternity it had seemed. The *Amity* experienced rough conditions and intense storms, which had forced temporary dockings on small islands and delayed the ship's arrival to the New World by weeks. Holme traveled with his four children, Hester, Thomas, and Tyrall nearly adults, the recently departed William Crispin's son, Silas, who was now in Holme's care and would be staying with the family in William Markhall's home in Pennsylvania in an area currently called New Castle, as well as Captain Diamond, fellow Quakers, and men who would be under Holme's commission as surveyor when they reached land. Penn remained in England for the time being, as he still had negotiations and dealings for this new province to oversee, but he had promised to join them within a year and act as governor of Pennsylvania. It was just as well, as Holme needed the time to properly survey the land and find Penn's city for brotherhood and sisterhood. The trip had made Holme ill several times, and fears arose that he was cursed to die on sea like the last surveyor, Crispin. Moreover, he feared what he would see if he did survive and they reached this new land. Stories were told of savage natives to this land who stalked the woods nearly naked besides loin cloths in the summer and animal furs and pelts in the winter. These natives, who were called Indians, had brown skin and were stern of visage, only showing their teeth when delivering the death blow with the ax or arrow, and had long, straight hair as black as pitch and covered their faces and bodies in oils and paint when out on the hunt or in war. They were said to strike in the dead of night or in the hidden passageways of the forest that the European man was ignorant of, and through their introduction to alcohol by such colonists, had grown even more savage and wild in nature; killing indiscriminately in the hopes for more of this elixir. Swedes and Germans trading cloths and blankets with them had also brought these Indians a pandemic of disease and decimated their numbers, leaving the surviving members with an intense hatred of the white man who was not only taking their land, but intentionally or unintentionally killing their kin. It would be Holme's responsibility to walk these woods of the New World and be wary of these natives that lurked in the shadows, but also to deal with them directly and reach some level of pacification. It would be, in fact, Holme's first duty to deliver Penn's letter to these Indians, the Lenni Lenape tribe of this area of America. Would they be receptive? Would they murder him there on the spot? He had been a soldier most of his adult life, but he was nearly sixty now, and these fit tribesmen, still hunters for survival and not sport, could pose a real threat. There were also said to be strange beasts in these lands, some innocuous forms of birds, rabbits, insects, and deer, to tales of dragons in the caves on the mountains, to devils and demons that had wiped out full colonies in the earliest days of settlement. If anything else, would there be adequate lodgings when they reached New Castle? There were houses and huts occupied by Swedish colonists, but would there be enough for his family and this ship full of people? Had he been a fool to trust this young, ambitious man Penn? He was an old widower and soldier, did he have the stamina for a new world? Could Penn really build this new society where they could worship freely and also accept and not persecute others' beliefs? Even so, would the king and English government eventually intercede and need to rule this world too?

The *Amity* reached port in New Castle on the 20th of June, and Holme stepped onto the lush and soft ground in relief, finally on earth with the floor not moving below his feet. The land was green for as long as he could see, with scores of trees in all directions. Somewhere in this warm, green, wooded land, Holme would need to find Penn's new Babylon, his Jericho, his Jerusalem of the New World.

Holem met with the Lenape three days after his arrival, Penn's letter, which he had rehearsed several times, firmly in his hands. The Swede Lasse Cock, who knew the Lenape language from being in the territory for several years, accompanied Holme as his translator. A few of Lord Baltimore's officials joined them as well, acting as guides and potential enforcement if the tribe was not receptive.

The Lenape were wary of the white man entering their town, so they agreed to meet on the banks of the Delaware River. The white man was their holocaust, and Holme, having been involved with these clashes of native and foreigners his whole life, prepared for the worst.

Holme looked upon the assembly of ten Indians, Chief Swapese at the head, and greeted them gravely. As he had imagined, they did wear loincloths of an impressive hyde, but were without any paints on their bodies or weapons. There was an elderly woman among the fit men who wore a European blouse and skirt, which shocked Holme. They were solemn of visage, and stared at Holme without expression. He was nervous, but hid it well with his deep, authoritative voice as he read Penn's letter to the tribe slowly, pausing for Lasse to translate. Penn acknowledged the Lenape were of the same origin under God, and vowed to be honest and fix any wrongdoings previous settlers inflicted on the people. At the conclusion of his reading, the people said not a word and withdrew into the forest.

Holme stalked all the forests and lands that spring from the Delaware River, searching for Penn's city. He was acute in any foreign sound to his ear in these woods, seeing squirrel and rabbit of unfamiliar species, and the eagle in the sky. He came across Lenape often as he surveyed the land, keeping his hand ready at his pistol trigger until the Indian walked away. They were shadows and ghosts at these woods, yet relatively harmless, if just unknown. Whom he really feared were the shiftless fur traders and brigands of these lands. They traveled in packs like wild dogs and were often without homes, living off swindling the Indian or muscling these religious refugees who were pacifists and generous of heart, falling for stories of winters of hardship and lost kin, only to let the brigands into their homes to be murdered or robbed in the dead of night. Holme felt a duty to be the protector of these people from the lawless of the New World.

He no longer believed in bloodshed, but he had seen it for too long to ever truly be redeemed, and would gladly go back into this sin in order to shield the innocent members of the Society of Friends. Holme even believed the devil himself could be somewhere in these trees, and he was prepared to put forth a fight.

He surveyed the creek the Lenape called the Pennypack, though Europeans called the Dublin Creek, and the Neshaminy Creek farther north. Holme assessed these lands to be prime for the city of Philadelphia, though as Penn arrived, he was redirected more towards the stretch of land situated between the Delaware River to its east and the Schuylkill River to its west. Still, he loved these lands that were soon constituted as Dublin Township. Holme felt a power and control unlike he had ever had in his life; a life of colonels barking orders or kowtowing blindly to kings. Now the lands were marked by his own eye and pen, and the names and layouts of the maps would remain. Holme was to have a great plantation built soon, a home where his whole family, sons-in-law, and grandchildren could stay. He even envisioned a grammar school for his grandchildren and the children of the newcomers who were arriving in droves. He thought of these wild, untamed lands as begging for order. He saw even blocks and a grid. He saw the Lenape wearing collared shirts, pants, and brimmed hats; square blocks, each symmetrical and ordered. Every man a king to his own, equal block. The spilled blood of kinsmen thousands of miles away. A society of friends for the futures, for his days were in the wane.

As he walked with great vigor for the days to come, a juggernaut of pain would press upon his heart, to the point where he could barely breathe and would have to rest at the closest stump or fallen log. He would think of Sarah, unable to share in this dream with him; he would think of Cromwell and Bradford and those wanton rulers and generals who thrust the blade in his hand. He remembered lining up Irish citizens and slaughtering them by the hundred. One pious fellow running his hands between his rosary beads before he fell. Admiral Penn strutting through the streets of Dublin and boasting of his feats at the local inn. Holme prayed in these moments until his thoughts were solely with the Lord and he was able to walk on.

Holme soon longed for these relatively peaceful hikes through the Pennypack woods, as his maps and allotments were being realized. His visions taking reality, and the thought was true of the final utopia, a city of brothers in love and in Christ, by a man nearly akin to a prophet or hero of the Bible, born and gained advantage through blood until nearly destructed, only to return with the boon of wealth, knowledge, and true zeal to not want, but need to forge a new, righteous path that did not do so through brute dominance, but intellect and compassion. Holme worked in Penn's council and eventually rose to justice of the peace. He was true in his rulings, but soon knew that such utopias were purely fictional works. He saw the Indian, not mere savage, but lover of the Earth, a proto-monk unlike he could fathom, who would pray to each item of the Earth before use, thanking the tree for its bark before chopping it down for a canoe or firewood, kissing each corn husk prior to the meal, using every inch of the animal, even its bones and being truly mournful to take its life so the Indian could live, into an unscrupulous glutton who raided camps and houses for liquor and murdered each other over the most trivial of altercations. He saw wives and young women brought before him and accused of witchcraft, males claiming poor crops were the result of magic or some type of devil worship. He listened to testimony from townspeople, and he despised himself for believing it true, for he knew that evil and the devil were real, but just how present were these tormentors? Was the devil the price we paid for this life of autonomy, this fertile and unblemished world? Was this former beautiful angel the true king of these lands, corrupting young, innocent puritan women to lay with him and serve in the ultimate corruption? There were miles and miles of untrodden land, but as he sat in his chamber, nearly seventy and seeing his world built before him, he knew that there was no such devil, no evil to be quantified in one spectacular being. The devil was this life, this hand of man. A life of conquests and righteousness that was always wrong to another. Others would always suffer for others to have the spoils. The only good in the world is the belief that you leave it slightly better than when you came. So he smashed down his gavel and denounced these witchcraft accusations and told them to speak and to think of such things no more, for you harvest as you plant, and if the wheat be golden praise it that day, and if the wheat be shriveled plant again and it will have life once more. Then he took off his robes and he returned to Well Spring Plantation to sit on his porch as the day crept away and called his servants from the field, who were good and loyal and never once complained and he looked upon his great estate in this new Dublin and wept as they gathered round him, for he knew of his life and the sin it held and this greatest sin of all to hold dominion over another man, though legal and in step with noble colonists, and he said to them, "I have lived longer than I should. The world will label or justify as it may, but I have done you a great unkindness, and I pray God will forgive my soul. When my day comes you will all be freed and rewarded for your service. Let your hearts rage, but rage for right. Let not these lands run rampant with tyranny, and do not by tyrannical in return. Walk the earth as the Indians, judge them not but learn of their kindness. Do not squabble with religion, but do as your heart knows to be true. I am sorry for my injustice, and soon enough, the Lord will judge me rightly."

And he passed in early April and was buried and marked by a stone with no description. His lands grew larger and a granite obelisk was erected in his name by the Crispin Athletic baseball fields with the Pennypack trees hanging above as cars pass by on Holme Avenue, each driver hoping to get a little further than they did the day before.

CHAPTER ELEVEN

There was a hard snowfall right after New Year's, and Michael Dempsey was asked by Al Mercer to work the early, early morning shift to plow the developments in Yardley. Mercer also asked Dempsey to recruit his sons for the job to shovel the walkways for ten dollars an hour until all was cleared. So, he and his sons got up at two AM, bundled up, and headed to the Philadelphia suburbs. It seemed promising to Connor. He enjoyed shoveling when he was younger, and he was growing a little stir crazy, on his winter break from freshman year, spending most nights staring at the caduceus on the cover of his nursing textbook, and doing nearly anything but opening it up and studying as he should. He would just daydream on the two weaving snakes vining up the staff and then facing each other at the top. What an odd image for health. Connor failed a class during the first semester, and he could feel the material slipping away from him, but he just could not bring himself to complete the task. He was weary of over twelve years of school already, and the freedom that college brought also made it that much easier not to do it. He didn't have priests breathing down his neck to get the assignments done. No father-this-and-that, no parents conferences or detention. Just his own foolishness for not doing what he was supposed to do. After all, his friends were home for break. It was time to drink at Heaven or Pollock or some other spot in Pennypack. Maybe, if they dared, they would even try Penny's or Hemmingway's with their fake I.D.s.

He was given the lecture many times: the one about how your brothers look up to you and you need to set a good example. Then his father would level with him and talk about all of the times when he was his age but also reverse course and talk about how he never quite got the chance to sow his oats since he was drafted and when he got back, everyone was older and with jobs or married and when hetried to get back to that previous state and then his dad got sick and that was about that for his youth. Connor wanted to show his brothers Kevin and John the right way, but it was hard when he didn't quite know it himself. He had this vague bitterness within him, as if he finally realized that he had been lied to for his entire life. Maybe not that severe, but some moment or chapter withheld from him. A mysterious illness when he was young? Struggles in school when he was very young that he could not quite recall. Saying "th-mart" rather than "smart". Looking at the words on the page and having no idea what they meant. It could have not have been sinister, but it just wasn't there. Maybe everyone felt the same way. Who's to say exactly how good a memory is supposed to be?

Since he had graduated high school, he refused to go to church until he went during one advent service at Saint Jerome's and received confession by Father Hughes because that was all his mother said she wanted from him for Christmas. He kneeled and awkwardly made the sign of the cross while the priest, the pastor of Saint Jerome's, sat facing forward in the pew in front of him and Connor said, "Bless me father, for I have sinned, it has been two months since my last confession and these are my sins," which in itself was a lie and a sin since it had been nearly a year since his last confession and Father Hughes listened patiently as Connor stated that he had been disrespectful to his parents and that he thought impure thoughts, which had been his standard confession since he was eight years old and Father Hughes said, "Mmm hmm," and nodded his head and asked Connor if there was anything else he would like to confess and Connor said, "No," and Father Hughes said, "These are grave sins, and I trust you are sorry for what you have done. We must love and respect our parents as Jesus loved and respected his mother and father. When we have impure thoughts, pray my son, for guidance and absolution. For your penance, please say three Hail Marys. Now, the Act of

Contrition," and Connor and Father Hughes said in unison, "Oh my God, I am heartily sorry for having offended Thee, and I detest all my sins because I dread the loss of Heaven and the pains of Hell. But most of all because they have offended Thee, my God, Who are all good and deserving of all my love." And he exited the church and saw Sister Fiscetti glaring at him, recalling in her mind how often she had seen him in church in the last year and he walked toward his Relient, certain he would only return for Christmas and Easter. He did not necessarily lose full faith or consider Jesus and the Bible full fabrication, but it was this confession. A constant search and admission of sin. A trapping of compounding guilt and infinite fallibility that seemed to make it all, life that is, futile. A birth waiting to die to finally be cleansed, perfect little angels. Why deny pleasure so? Why confine your body to one uniform every day, with the same cross and Latin phrase in its emblem? Why hear the same gospel passages at the same intervals in the same masses that you have been brought to since before you could speak or even comprehend speech? Why recite the same prayers asking God for forgiveness for just existing? He had finally seen glimmers of the actual world in his college prerequisites and English class. Religions of the world that made just as much sense, or more sense, than the one he had been told since birth would lead him to heaven. He read authors unafraid and unapologetic in seeing the world in a different way, some hundreds of years before television or internet. It all helped reinforce that there was something out there to find. Something beyond Philadelphia house and Irish Catholic girl and mass every Sunday and 3-5 kids. Still, he was afraid. He wanted this zest, this wild abandon to live in the ephemeral and not repent afterwards, but it was not gone, this guilt, this Saturday morning hanging your head in shame for getting too drunk the night before and not quite remembering every moment and seeing a cut on your palm and ankle and not quite knowing how it got there and your mom saying cryptically "Did you have fun last night?" and your dad, more bluntly, saying. "You need to cut this shit," and being more terrified by how you may have acted around your buddies and what they're going to reveal to you when you go out with them Saturday night to do it all again.

Connor entered the front passenger seat of the Mercer Lawn Care truck with his father driving and his brothers Kevin and John in the back. His father revved the white Ford 150 with the Mercer decals and attached plow to the grill, and they drove off into the darkness.

The Yardley suburban development was covered in white. His father would have to plow and remove the snow from the streets and cul-de-sacs until there was only asphalt to be seen. Connor and his brothers were given shovels and began working on the sidewalks and driveways. The weather was frigid, but they were all dressed in layers and rather warm once they began working. Kevin was two years younger than Connor, and John nearly four. Kevin was on the crew team for his first two years at Judge, but quit after the fall season because he couldn't get in a boat. The sport had made him fairly muscular, and he continually showed it by heaving the shoveled snow just a little bit farther than everyone else. He was also pretty heavy in music, specially Creedence and Grateful Dead, and had been playing guitar more frequently lately. There were rumors that he smoked cigarettes now, but he swore it was only once or twice just to try it. Kevin was much like Burke in those ways--a boy for another time. He and Connor used to fight like wild men when they were younger, but they had begun to get along once they were both in high school. John was most like his father, in that the line was always hard work and sports. John, as a freshman, had already had a job working at the Saint Jerome's rectory, doing the occasional secretarial job for the priests and parish, but also landscaping and maintaining the parish greens. He had something akin to a stone face, grimacing like a moai statue on Easter Island or Michaelangelo's Moses. He was a driven kid, and Connor was proud of him. Yet, John also made him frustrated in a sense because looking at John was like looking at himself a few years prior. A locked human just waiting for people to please and rules to follow. The fear in his brother's otherwise steely eyes of failure and disappointing another. Even tonight, as his dad informed him of getting up a two AM, he did not even give the slightest sigh. He just said, "Okay, Dad," went to bed for a few hours, got dressed, and was ready to go.

The first hour went quickly, and Connor was pleased to be doing the work. He was not cold, and he could feel his dormant muscles coming back to life. He was active in sports in high school, playing CYO and even reffing some basketball games from time to time, but his first college semester seemed consumed with nothing but studying, essays, and drinking. His essay writing had actually turned out to be a strong suit of his, as he got an A on nearly every written assignment, and his paper of the Federalist Papers was even highlighted by the professor during one of the lectures. Connor struggled mightily with writing in high school, but now it all suddenly seemed to click.

The second hour brought slight fatigue, and Kevin started to moan about being tired and hungry. Connor felt the same way, but he had to be the big brother, he figured, so he told him to shut up, they would feed them soon enough. John grunted in agreement and they shoveled on. Connor was now sweating and took off his jacket and just wore his hoodie. He didn't see his father, or Al Mercer, or any other supervisors, which worried him slightly, with a faint fear that they were here all alone. He willed himself to think otherwise, as he thought of how long this job was slated for--over ten hours. It would be hard work, but he needed hard work. He needed money. And, he and his brothers were Michael's kids; Al or someone would pull up any moment with a truck full of pizzas or hoagies, they would feast and get an hour break, and then return to the job reinvigorated.

By the fourth hour, they were all starving and exhausted. They pushed the shovel into the heavy snow, lifted and tossed by rote memory. Connor's face felt blistered by the cold winds and sweat that was drying on his brow and lips. Connor was proud of what he and his brothers had accomplished so far, and there was some manliness to the endeavor--something about testing your will against the elements and the plethora of physical pain, and still standing and not even complaining too much really, just doing your job. That was at least something he had, and his brothers too, this grit, this unrivaled competitiveness and resolve. Burke or McNamara would probably have quit hours ago, lit cigarettes, and walked until they found a Septa bus or could hitch a ride. It must have been something their father taught them-- putting your head down and going to work. What could be a better representation of such drive, digging and tossing until the man tells you you don't have to do that any more.

At nearly hour six, a Mercer truck arrived, and the three boys dropped their shovels and ran to it, believing it to be their father come to save them. However, as they got closer and the truck window rolled down, it revealed Al Mercer's son, Al Mercer Jr. He was about ten years older than Connor, though the acne on his face and measly facial hair made him appear like an adolescent. Al was somewhat of a burnout, delivering pizza at Salvito's, still living at home, and even still smoking weed and drinking 40s at Pollock from time to time. His parents were divorced, and from what Connor recalled, he lived with his mother.

"We're trying to get you guys fed," Al announced groggily from the truck, "but every place we've tried is closed with the snow and all. It's early still; I'm sure something will be open soon. Just hang tight and keep at it."

"Where's our dad?" Connor asked.

"He's somewhere over on Chestnut--over in Newtown. A pretty big job there, so we needed him to supervise. I'll be back around." And Al drove off and they were alone again.

It was nearly ten AM, and the hunger, cold, and fatigue truly set in. It was funny, how in all of these houses in the development, not one resident came out of their beautiful single houses to ask "How are you doing?" let alone offer the brothers hot chocolate or a bite to eat. The thought of money for this job left Connor's mind, and his mind seared red in anger. He hated his dad for putting him and his brothers out here and never returning. He hated the Mercers for never giving them a respite, and he hated most of all these rich snobs sitting comfortably in their pajamas sipping their coffee and eating their breakfast on their marble breakfast nooks, looking out with quiet contempt at Connor, a lowly worker who was not worthy of such luxuries. One day he would have a home even larger, he told himself. I will be the one paying for the service. I will be the great one--and he thought about what that greatness would be. Sure, he could make decent money as an RN, but it wasn't about being an RN. No one ever remembered what an RN did. What could this be? He wasn't talented in music like his brother. He couldn't act or do anything like that. All he knew was that he had a greatness in him. A legacy. A story that needed to be told. Maybe he was going delirious, but in a brief moment it was all so lucid. People talking about him as being a genius. Fawning over some book where he could almost see the cover art, and he could almost see the title, and in a spark the story was there, but then John started talking about the Flyers and he lost that thought and heaved another lump of snow on another lump of snow.

By one PM all sensations were evaporated from his body. He moved the shovel without even feeling it in his hands nor the weight of the snow as he pushed it. His brothers kept asking him questions which they knew he did not have an answer:"Where is Dad? When can we finish? Where is everyone else? Is someone going to feed us? Are we stuck here?" these vain questions irritated him beyond a response, and it was almost as if they were saying such things because the barrier between internal and external speech had been broken, and either delirium or a last ditch effort for sanity was taking hold. It may as well have been the artic, this suburban cul-de-sac with every 4-5 bedroom house and two SUVs in the driveway. The thought continued to escalate in his mind to just bang on a door and beg the owner, if he had any human decency, to let him and his brothers in and feed them and keep them warm.

The sun was now oppressively bright, reflecting off the mounds of snow and now taking another sense away from Connor. Finally, as he was finishing shoveling a driveway, he saw the Mercer Lawn Care truck pull up, Al Jr. driving and his father in the passenger seat. His father could barely look at him as they approached.

"Your pop hurt his back over in Newtown," Al stated bluntly as he took a drag of his cigarette. "We were gonna take him to the hospital, but he thinks he's all right."

"I'm sorry, boys," Michael said weakly, barely audible.

"A resident found him on his front law laid out. Be thankful we're not thawing your dad out right now," he chuckled and motioned to the truck bed. "Hop in the back. I'm taking yous home."

Connor and his brothers rode in the bed, holding tightly to the edged. The cold air stung his face. It was almost fitting that after hours alone in the cold outdoors, he couldn't even ride inside of a car home.

He found himself staring at the back of his father's head as they rode. There were still small chunks of ice in his salt and pepper hair, and his father was starting to develop a bald spot his father probably didn't even know about. He could not see his father's face, but he knew he was in pain. He wriggled every minute or so, and his hand gripped at his vertebrate, as if he could catch and snuff out the tormenting sensation. After pulling up at the house, Connor and his brothers helped carry their father in and laid him down on his bed. There is such a cruelty that comes with life. That a man works hard enough to just one day have that work break him in two, and then you are no longer useful and you must go away.

*

Tara Dempsey slid her fingers back and forth across the image of Our Lady of Mount Carmel appearing to Simon Stock on the front square of her scapular, while the back square which rested on her spine read "Whoever dies clothed in this scapular shall not suffer eternal fire" and she looked down on her husband, who was finally resting after writhing in bed with his back pain. It had happened at last, the work had broke him, and she figured it would break her too one of these days. The only thing there seemed was this faith. She would have otherwise crumbled years ago. How else was there to deal with the death. To see people breather their last breaths nearly weekly. How could it have been as simple as life created, life ended, and then buried or incinerated, cut open and plucked of any final usefulness if young enough. The stories were to myriad to all be false--of Jesus with his disciples--why would they have laid down their lives if they weren't certain, or knew that Heaven awaited? How about the miracles? Padre Pio? The Saints, intervening and curing the impossible--it was almost as frequent as the deaths witnessed, medical procedure and medicine used to its conclusion, the patient given Last Rites, and then they wake up good as new the next day. How could it not be true? With all of her years pouring through textbooks and medical encyclopedias, wasn't there something greater that held it all together? Believe in the medicine, believe in those that create and administer it, but believe in that invisible hand weaving it all. It was nice to have this faith, to believe, to wear the medallions, pray the prayers, attend the masses, and receive the Host, but it was still difficult when it came to Michael, to see him there, hobbled, made her realize the mortality of all. When he was twenty-six, twenty-seven, he would never die. His flat stomach lounging on a beach chair in Ocean City, smoking the occasional cigar and twisting the bottle cap from the beer. Hauling mounds of sod and mulch across her parents' lawn, carrying a bookshelf up the stairs singlehandedly of their newly purchased house--that first bill a nearly unfathomable number, and now the house finally paid off. That work. That God--that damn work. Tara and Michael pushing the car payments back. Michael with his head down low asking her father for a small loan. The tuition going up at Saint Jerome's, the boys wanting the latest action figures or video game system. Opening new credit card accounts. She working holidays for double pay just so she could afford the present she couldn't be there to see opened. Fatih. Pray. Be patient. God has a plan. He gives you what you can take.

Work. She, seven, waiting with her older brother and younger sister in the den--all staring at the fake brick facade on the wall and the clock with the mini elm trees on the sides of the face. Waiting for it to reach 5:30 and her father to slam the door open and her mother in her gravely, tobacco-torn voice, rattling off all of their children's misdeeds of the day and she hearing her father's belt buckle unhinge and the leather belt gliding off of his slacks and the snap of the belt like the wind howling and her older brother Tommy saying, "Say your prayers" like a cowboy because he'd been hit so many times and it no longer hurt but she still thought maybe Daddy is just playing a trick, like he did that one time on Easter and put the belt down and gave us all Peanut Chew chocolates but then he came in and he was not playing a trick and whipped her on the ass and she cried a little differently each time.

But that's what they did back then and at least she vowed to never do the same to the boys and she kept her vow. And so she resigned herself in the acceptance of burden, because at some point all of the welts and yelling made her tough and it was at least her duty to take what the world needed of her and try to bring it some kindness in return, and she was not bitter that Connor had lost his faith the moment he left Father Judge and would often make little, freshman in college, speeches about the hypocrisy of religion and how it only brings division and suffering and that God does not create man, man creates God, and through that elegance of speech that came through her reading to him every night and hiring tutors when they told him he could not read and those twelve years of education paid through witnessing and guiding people into death which shook her so much religion was the only thing left, she was unable to articulate back to him just how truly important it was and he would most likely never understand.

Michael laid on the bed with his eyes closed, doing his best to feign sleep. The pain in his back was too severe to sleep anyway, but he did not have the ability to see the world at this time. He had failed his sons severely. They were in the cold, tired and hungry. He was stiff on a mound of snow, trying his best to move but completely immobilized and helpless. They all must despise me now, he surmised. I have lead them all astray, and now we're doomed. It was embarrassing, it truly was. You live until you're the butt of the joke. The pathetic nonentity that everyone needs to keep alive. Tara will fuss over me and treat me like a king. I won't want her to do it, but she will. She is a blessing. Why don't I tell her enough? That time passed somehow; we haven't had that for a while. It's something like a working partnership. Damnit, why can't we go back--we can. I'll get this back taken care of, fixed up, and good as new, and then, hell, we'll just go on a date--and I'll kiss her on the lips like I used to and tell her how lovely she is every chance that I get. I must do better. I must.

CHAPTER TWELVE

So this is a real college, Dempsey thought to himself cynically as he parked his Relient around 16th and Cecil B. Moore Avenue and walked toward Burke and McNamara's dorm in Temple University. The blocks off campus were a smattering of collegiate pizza shops and bars, bookstores, and tiny neighborhood bodegas, breakfast joints straight from the 1950s, and hole-in-the-wall dive bars that would scare the piss out of anyone not from the city to step into. Cecil B. Moore intersected with Broad Street, which ran straight down to city hall, the old gothic and Greco-Roman building with the iron statue of William Penn on top, the liberty tower skyscrapers and other buildings which now shadowed the noble Quaker proprietor with his hand flatly stretched out at his waist.

Dempsey had a bottle of Captain Morgan in his backpack, and he was excited to finally be shown around campus and pre-game in the dorms, and then party at a house off campus. He stepped onto Temple's campus, and it was suddenly no longer North Philadelphia, but the safe refuge for young scholars. Every person was different in their own way, and yet all happy--like walking into Oz, but with a cherry brick road as opposed to a golden one. The college even had its own police force with officers on bicycles and alert stations every hundred yards or so--even an old cop driving a little golf cart around. The air of the university screamed that the week of studying was over, and even if there was an 8 AM class, we would be drinking tonight.

Burke and McNamara's dorm was on the corner of Liacouras Walk and Norris. Dempsey was warned that the security would be checking backpacks at the front desk, as drinking in the dorms was prohibited, so Dempsey went into the alleyway of the west side of the dorm, and saw Burke flagging him down from a fourth floor window. With gesturing akin to Navy Seals, Burke began to slowly lower a rope from the window to Dempsey. A few people from other floors began to look out of their windows in confusion and then begin to laugh at this absurd operation. Dempsey double-knotted the rope to the handle of his backpack, saluted Burke, and then Burke hauled up the treasure.

"We'll call it the umbilical cord," Burke stated after signing Dempsey in and they walked upstairs. The halls were nearly brand new, brightly lit, with white walls and berber carpet. Burke's floor even had a pool table and vending machines. Dempsey was envious that he was not here with them, and with his grades teetering in the C-D range, it would be a longshot to complete nursing school at Temple anyway. The thought passed by the time he reached Burke's dorm, and he thought only of drinking and being with his boys.

Burke had a minifridge filled with Schmidt's cans, which had bears and salmon on the labels for some reason. Burke's wall was covered with posters of his heroes. The iconic Jim Morrison shirtless, Bob Dylan looking away and holding a bass guitar, and the typical Led Zeppelin "Stairway to Heaven" with the old monk on the cliff holding the lantern, and the "Dark Side of the Moon" poster--the single white light entering the prism and a rainbow shooting out of the other end. Burke also had a record player, which was currently spinning "Deja Vu" by Crosby, Stills, Nash, and Young. Dempsey took out the bottle of Captain Morgan and placed it on Burke's desk. Without a word, Burke grabbed dixie cups from the bathroom and when McNamara arrived, the three cheersed to Pollock and gulped the whiskey down and then began drinking the Schmidt's, or Every-Other-Letter-Beer, as Burke called it.

"I tell you about the other night, Demps?"

Dempsey shook his head.

"McNamara wanted to play at this open mic on South Street, and we must have gotten off at the wrong stop or took the wrong train because we ended up in Northern Liberties or Fishtown, and we were just wandering--freezing cold with McNamara and his guitar on his back, and some bum came up to us. I was pretty drunk at this point and this guy asks for change. I don't know--I start mouthing off to him, and he pulls out a damn wrench--like a mechanic's wrench--and starts swinging it at me. Holy Shit, we ran so fast and hopped on the first Septa bus we saw and it took us to Chinatown. McNamara missed his open mic, but this place had bangin' lo mein, and they let us drink there. We split a carafe of saki and I puked it all up a minute later in the street. Oh man, so we grabbed a cab home and we both didn't have any money, so we bolted out as soon as the cabbie pulled over. Dude was screaming at us all the way down Broad Street."

They all laughed and McNamara continued, "You gotta see me during an open mic. I've been writing all of this new stuff. I've really got down how to sing and play at the same time. I even play harmonica while I'm playing guitar on a few songs."

"He's good man. You gotta come. Plus, the owner is a retired narc and he doesn't care if we drink underage."

"Burke really got me into Bob Dylan. He is such a genius. I never liked him before, but then I heard 'Tangled Up in Blue' and it all clicked for me. Some of the songs, I really get, you know. Anyway, I'm gonna go smoke a cigarette, wanna join?"

"I gotta get a shower. Some of the girls from the east wing will be coming over in a little bit," Burke said and already made his way to the bathroom.

"I'll have one,"Dempsey said and followed McNamara into the courtyard. Dempsey was not a smoker, but he liked the extra rush of a cigarette when drinking.

"That song 'Tangled Up in Blue', man," McNamara reflected after exhaling. He now wore a suede blazer with leather patches at the elbows, and his hair was now grown over his ears. "I really relate to that song."

"Oh yeah?"

"Yeah, the whole song he's talking about a girl who is just out of his reach: 'Her folks they said our lives together, sure was gonna be rough. They never did like mama's homemade dress, papa's bankbook wasn't big enough...We'll meet again some day on the avenue...I seen a lot of women, but she never escaped my mind and I just grew, tangled up in blue.' That's like me, man. I feel what he is saying there. I met a girl a few weeks ago right here on Liacouras Walk. Burke and I were drunk, causin' all hell, and Burke said something stupid to her, I don't even remember what, and then he rolled back into the dorms. I apologized for him and I started talking to her. I admit I was just trying to get with her at first, but she was like so sweet and patient. Such a cute, tiny voice and these eyes like a Disney princess or something. Ah man, I don't know--she lives in the dorm right over there. She says she has a boyfriend back home in Lansdale, but I don't know, sometimes they're together, sometimes they're not. I just feel like the guy in the song. I know she's meant for me, but it's just not happening. And then, the song, he says, 'Then she opened up a book of poems and handed it to me, written by an Italian poet, from the thirteenth century, and every one of them words rang true and glowed like burning coal, pouring off of every page, like it was written in my soul from me to you.' That's Petrach he's talking about I'm pretty sure--unrequited love, the doe, in the woods and the hunter. I don't know what to do."

"It'll work out. She's come around."

Demspey inhaled the last bit of cigarette and then flicked it out of the courtyard and walked with McNamara back inside. Burke was just stepping out of the shower when they returned and proudly swung his long wet hair back and forth, and then dressed. A moment later the girls from the east wing entered with a box of Franzia wine. Dempsey was amazed by how easy it all was-- to live in a building with girls who just come into your room and drank with you. If he attempted to bring a girl home, he would have to tiptoe with her through the basement and lightly up the stairs to his room and pray his mom or dad wouldn't hear the bed creek or her moan. One of the girls was Samantha, who went to Nazareth Academy in the Northeast, but he didn't know prior. Burke described her as quiet when sober but a wild woman after a few beers or wine. She had a firm body with large breasts and round ass that jiggled when she swayed to "Almost Cut My Hair". Burke said they had made out at a frat party a few weeks back, but things had not progressed beyond that. She seemed to be a little buzzed already and slurred slightly when she explained the girls had two shots in their dorm prior to arriving. Samantha's friend and roommate was Laura, a slightly plump girl from Reading. She wasn't as brazen as Samantha, and was timidly sitting on Burke's bed nursing a cup of wine. She had thick square glasses and wore a Led Zeppelin shirt of the Swan Song logo and a pair of jeans with rips in the knees. Her hair was brown with a few streaks of blonde--the remnants of an old highlighting job. She was in the Tyler College of Art, and was said to draw tremendous charcoal sketches of horses. She even had one back home named Gus. The third girl from the east wing was Jocelyn. She was short and petite, just under five feet tall, and had short blonde hair, nearly buzzed on the sides. She was from Moorestown, New Jersey, and she was going to school for accounting. Jocelyn had these sharp eyes that revealed an ever-present intelligence, not just seeing but processing and analyzing constantly. She was looking at Samantha as if looking for some pattern in her movement-- the swaying of Samantha's hips and the way she clutched her wine cup as some deeper repression being subtly revealed and becoming more obvious with each sip of alcohol she took. Dempsey saw this predator, this hunter in Jocelyn, and needed to find out more. He sat beside her and filled her cup with more wine.

"Nothing but the best here," he remarked.

"I'm a classy gal. When I drink wine from a box, it needs to be Franzia."

"I'm the same way with my beer. If it doesn't have a wild animal on the can, then I'm out!"

"Here's to like minds!" and they cheered.

"So you're not afraid of needles?"

"What's that?"

"You're going to be a nurse, right?"

"Oh, yeah. I haven't had to do anything like that yet, just

really learned CPR so far, but I'll be okay."

"You need to hurt someone to help someone. It's funny how that works."

"That's true. I feel it only hurts if someone looks at it though. If they look away, it's really not that bad. Just a little pinch."

"So that's what you recommend, looking away?"

"Yeah, it always hurts when you see it coming."

"Yo, so let's head over to the party at 16th and Norris in about an hour," Burke interrupted, "It's some of my boys from my Intellectual Heritage class," and then directed them over to his desk to take a shot of Captain Morgan.

Dempsey went to the fridge and grabbed another Schmidt's. McNamara was there to meet him.

"You're always pretty good with girls, man. What do you think I should do? Should I call her to see if she wants to go to this party?"

"If you want. It's worth a shot."

"Okay. Nah I mean, maybe she'll be there or I'll see her out. It'll be much better that way."

"How so?"

"It'll be meant to be, that's how it has to go. That's destiny and everything like that."

"Whatever you think."

"Oh man, this sucks. Last Sunday, I could not go to sleep at all. My mind was racing and I was dead sober. I kept thinking about her and how unfair it was that she had a boyfriend and that dude probably treats her like shit. Ah, the thoughts just kept coming. So then, I really just started to shut my eyes, and they were just about closed but I could still see out, and, I swear to God man, I saw ghosts hovering over me and waving their hands in my face like seeing if I was awake. So I would open my eyes more and they vanished. Then I closed my eyes again and same thing. The ghosts reappeared with their hands in my face and they had like long dreadlocks and were young and then my eyes were fully opened and everything really started to rush in. A deluge of thoughts about my own death and what will happen when I die and what comes after that if there is even a heaven, do we just stay there forever and why does she have a boyfriend and I could feel my heart pressing against my chest and then I just heard a voice say, "Give it time."

"Give it time?"

"Yeah, give it time and that's what I've been thinking. Just have patience and it will work. Don't look at me like I'm crazy."

"Ah man, McNamara with the ghost sightings," Burke interjected.

"I couldn't believe it myself. I still can't believe it, but it happened. I don't really know what else to say, like maybe that's how it happens. No one believes until the unbelievable happens. Um, I need a cigarette," and he stepped to the window and smoke and Burke joined him. Connor continued to talk to Jocelyn and felt he was flirting fairly well. She would not be easy, and she reveled in challenging him as far as he could tell. He was feeling good and confident. His blonde curly hair and blue eyes were irresistible. He was going to be a nurse; he cared for people; he was witty and could match her volleys. He could look at her and not reveal fully his captivation with her delicate eyes and small freckles that diffused from the corners of her eyes down her soft cheeks and even a stray freckle making its way all the way down her full, rubicund lips. He wanted to touch her. He wanted to tell her some truth, but it was much too early in the game. He had to be cool, unaffected, and subtly inch closer and make a tiny, innuendo and--

"What are you looking at? Hey, yeah, keep walking you fuckin' pussy! Yeah--wait--what's that--" Burke was yelling down from the window.

"Assholes, stay down there!" McNamara continued.

Dempsey joined them at the window to see the group of a few guys they were yelling at. They were all wearing jeans and golf shirts, most likely on their way to a party. One of the guys halted his friends and lifted his middle finger right at Burke.

"Fuck it, let's go down," Burke said as he finished the rest of his beer and made his way downstairs, Demspey and McNamara following.

The four were waiting for them at the corner of Liacouras Walk and Norris, next to a closed food truck. The supposed leader wore a green striped golf shirt and confidently stepped forward.

"You should find better things to do then yell at people from your window...Smoking is bad for you too."

"Real tough guy, I'm sure. C'mon man, one on one," Burke implored and put up his fists. The other three boys and Dempsey and McNamara stepped away to give the two space. Like a banshee, Burke lunged at green golf shirt, who seemed pretty built, and didn't make contact. Green golf shirt ducked out of the way and connected on the side of Burke's head. This made Burke more angry, and he dove at green golf shirt and swung with both fists. One punch hit him on the shoulder, but green golf shirt now had hold of Burke's sweatshirt, punched Burke three consecutive times in the face, Burke's hair flinging backwards on impact.

"The fuckin' hippie can't fight," a kid in a blue golf shirt exclaimed. At this, Dempsey charged him and tackled him to the ground while punching. Blue golf shirt now on the ground, trying to get free, but Dempsey swinging downward furiously landing punch after punch. A blur of rage, Dempsey kept swinging until he was also tackled and his face slammed onto a sewer grate, and a moment later a knee in his back and his hands being twisted backwards and the cold metal cuffs on his wrist. As he was pulled up, he tasted the blood in his mouth, dripping from a gash above his lips. He looked down to see his blood on the metal grate, drizzling down into the darkness and a puddle of dark red on his sweatshirt. A moment later he was placed inside the police car and taken to Temple Hospital.

The fluorescent light burned on his skin as he sat in the waiting room of the hospital wit the police officer sitting next to him. He wondered what had happened to Burke and McNamara. Had they been arrested? Did they get away? The officer didn't say a word to him, just speaking in code into his walkie-talkie. It was stupid, and his lip was busted badly, but he had to do it. Something in him took over, and he was all beast. He was fighting for his clan, his brotherhood--no one could beat his friend or say his friend was a pussy. It didn't matter the pain he felt now, what the repercussion would be, he had to do it for Burke. He would have done it for him.

When it was time, the nurse washed the blood off of his face with a cloth, swabbed his skin numb, and injected a needle in the skin above his upper lip several times until he felt nothing, and sewed his wound shut with seven stitches. The officer drove him back to the dorm and issued him a citation for disorderly conduct. Burke met him at the security to sign him back in again and just said "Jesus Christ" as he saw Dempsey with his blood-stained sweatshirt and thick, black stitches above his mouth.

"What a first night at Temple, eh?" Burke said and laughed as he whomped Dempsey on the back. Burke somehow had no marks on him.

"I don't think they'll let me step foot on campus again."

"Hey, they will man! They need an RN with some first-hand experience."

"I guess I can confidently say what stitches feel like now."

"Exactly. Hey, the girls are back in the dorm, and we still have a bunch of beer. You have earned every drop my friend."

"Thanks."

When Connor returned to the dorm, he saw McNamara sitting at the desk in the corner with a cup of wine and the bottle of Captain Morgan. About one-third of the rum remained and McNamara was bragging that he had been drinking it straight from the bottle with no chaser. He was more at ease than earlier in the night, but he did not appear to be wasted quite yet. Dempsey, after the fight, arrest, and hospital visit, was feeling completely sober by now. Burke informed him that the group still went to the party, but police came shortly after and forced everyone out. As Dempsey entered, Samantha, Laura, and Jocelyn each took their turn in viewing the stitches on his face, holding his chin and turning his head as if he was some work of art and asking him "How long will you have the stitches and will it scar?" and

Dempsey not sure if they examined him in pity or curiosity, or if the act and consequential evidence made him more attractive in their minds. Either way, he had resolved in his mind to sleep with one of them as some type of twisted recompense for a disastrous start to the evening.

Burke and the girls grew bored, so they went to the local dive bar Lamar's where they knew they wouldn't get carded. McNamara stayed behind as he said he was getting tired. Lamar's was like a preserved 1970s joint, with one box TV in the corner behind the bar, old pull tab cans lining the walls, a dilapidated pool table with a strip of felt worn away, and only two other middle-aged black men slumped over their beers. With all of that drabness, it was still an exhilarating feeling to be drinking in a bar.

The group took a round of Southern Comfort shots, and Burke put a few songs on the jukebox. The girls began dancing and dempsey indiscriminately danced with all three. Jocelyn grinded onto him and reached her hand back and held his thigh. He moved his hands along her hips and up toward her chest. In a flash he turned her around and kissed her. She had played the cold, cunning intellectual earlier, but that veil was now lifted. She saw him as animal, as this wild force pulsating on instinct and not even caring about his own preservation. Brave or stupid, but attractive nonetheless. They kissed hard and sloppily in this dive bar until she said, "I'm going to the restroom," and he let her go for a minute and then went in and joined her, his stitches nearly ripped out by the time it was all over.

When Burke and Dempsey returned to the dorm, McNamara was passed out on the bed, still fully clothed with his sneakers on. As Dempsey went over to take McNamara's sneakers off, he noticed McNamara was not breathing. Panicked, Dempsey began to perform CPR on his friend, trying his best to remember every procedure learned. After a few intervals, McNamara came to and started talking gibberish. Relieved, Dempsey and Burke slowly stood him up and took him to the bathroom. While there, they forced McNamara, who was completely incapacitated, to throw up into the toilet. That brought McNamara to better cognizance, so they took his clothes off and put him in the shower to help sober him up. When he was done in the shower, Dempsey put sweats on him and laid him back into the bed. McNamara, with his eyes closed, softly repeated, "Give it time," until he fell back asleep and Dempsey soon followed.

CHAPTER THIRTEEN

Dempsey rode in the back of the school bus that, on this Saturday, contained drunken adults in green t-shirts, temporary shamrock tattoos on their faces, Irish flag suspenders, and tweed jeff caps, as opposed to children. It was the Shamrock Shuttle for Saint Patrick's Day, and the bus was its own transportation service to local Northeast Philadelphia bars for a mere five dollars. It was also a great opportunity to drink without being carded, as the bars in Holmesburg and Mayfair were swept up in the madness of hordes of people drunkenly celebrating their Irish heritage, or at least pretending to for the day. Dempsey thought about his own Irish roots, which really didn't extend too far beyond his grandmother watching the Notre Dame Fighting Irish whenever they were on, listening to Perry Como sing "When Irish Eyes are Smiling", or correcting people who said Saint Patty's Day to respect the name of Saint Patrick. Dempsey wished for something a little deeper than that, some family tree that extended to the earliest clans, but it was all nebulous as far as he knew. Besides not having any deeper meaning, this was truly a good day. Burke sat in front of him in the bus banging on the seat to some rhythm he had in his head and sipping from his dad's flask. McNamara was across the aisle staring out of the window. They began the day at Burke's parents' house at eight AM with some kegs and eggs, where Burke invited about twenty other friends and served scrambled eggs and hashbrowns along with some Natty Light. By eleven, they made their way to Out of Wack Jack's, played some shuffleboard and darts, and Dempsey got with some random blonde who sidled up next to him while he was ordering a drink, rubbed his chest, and then stuck her tongue down his throat. He had hopes of seeing her again at some point during the bar tour, but if he didn't, he was sure another girl would come along. That had been the norm nearly every night out now: one or two actions, a dance or a compliment, and he was making out or getting laid. He could do nothing but smile the whole time, just riding this awesome wave of drinking and women.

The bus stopped at Cottman and Frankford in Mayfair and they first went to Reale's. The DJ was blasting music and the bar was a wall-to-wall sea of green. Dempsey squirmed his way to a bartender, got a Miller, and joined his friends outside. He found himself fixated on McNamara, who was smoking a cigarette and generally not saying much today. McNamara caught Dempsey's gaze in return. Dempsey thought of how lucky that bastard was to have him as a friend, to have his life saved. McNamara was not breathing, his mouth just agape with no air coming out, eyes rolled in the back of his head. Did he really know how close he was to being dead? And McNamara thinking of that night and having such devastation over his lack of memory. To be told, "Hey, you could have died," and not knowing anything about it was frightening. He just woke up the next day, saw vomit on his shirt and on the ground and realized he was five minutes late for his World Religions exam, took the multiple choice, handed it into the professor, went into the bathroom and vomited, and then came back and completed his written responses. Like a jigsaw puzzle, finding clues from the night--an empty bladder of boxed wine, an empty bottle of Captain Morgan and slugging the bottle down as if it were a beer, getting in some type of fight, talking about ghosts, and nearly dying. It had scarred him certainly, but also instilled in him a greater resolve, a greater belief that he, McNamara, was here for some greater purpose. He had survived a night wandering the slums with a guitar on his back, he had survived a pouncing by a horde of twenty-five-year-olds after mouthing off at a bar in Conshohocken. His vision was so damn bright. He saw the songs about to be written. He saw a marriage and kids to Sarah Rahleigh. He was a child of destiny, a quiet dark horse who would ascend above it all. It was in this rapture that he loved Dempsey, but there was no way that he could express it properly. No precedent to walk over, kiss him on the cheek, thank him, and truly share his gratitude. Before he was truly out of his haze, Burke tapped him on the shoulder and directed him to Harrington's down the block.

It was an unseasonably warm mid-March day, and Burke was thrilled to be part of it all. McNamara followed him faithfully, and began talking about a newly discovered Cat Stevens song he had found. It was a fun past-time, talking to McNamara about this-or-that almost hidden artist or band. He would bring up an obscure T-Rex tune, McNamara would counter with "Panic in Detroit" from Diamond Dogs, and so on. McNamara had the talent; he played guitar and produced these riffs and chord progressions that could be songs on the radio, but somehow felt to Burke like the follower, Burke's toady. He had the chops, Burke was just an underachiever with a set of ears. This seemed most apparent in Mcnamara's smoking and drinking habits now. McNamara was a kid who wouldn't touch liquor in high school, and now he had almost drank himself to death. He was a kid who would busboy on weekends and get up early on Saturdays for a run through Pennypack Park, now he was smoking a pack a day and sleeping until noon most days. Burke felt himself as the great corruptor in a way. They were all going down, and they were following his lead. He, a twisted shepherd who took his flock into the depths of the valleys, where his staff and his legs were strong enough to take them to the highest peaks, to fear no predator and live in peace. Ah, but to lead you must be more protector than hunter--yes, you must know how that stalker thinks, and when it will strike, but you must be fully resolved to step in front of the weakest of the flock when the beast emerges from the darkness with its ravenous jaws and jagged teeth with saliva frothing and spilling onto the earth. He was not that leader yet, but his flock was ready to believe when he opened his mouth and pointed his finger and jutted out his chest that real fury would follow, but as of now, it had not. He gave only weak punches that were swallowed by opponents, and then laughed at and pummeled in return, like a reoccuring nightmare of swinging his fist with maximum force, only to have it slowed as if punching through a blob of hard gelatin, and when the punch finally makes its way through it barely grazes the combatant and the combatant, always faceless yet all, simply walks away. Somewhere in him was that chubby, straight A student, eighth grader. The one who stayed after school to work on algebraic concepts and complete equations in Math Club. The one who had an article in the Northeast Times about his scholarship and his buddies teasing him about his awkward smile while holding the check and the "Wizard of Winchester Park" article headline about that picture and everyone calling him Wiz until his eighth grade graduation from Saint Jerome's. The one who seemed to hit puberty a click later than the other boys and entered Father Judge with his cherubic face and buzzcut while everyone else had at least a peach-fuzz mustache. And then his dad got the pair of boxing gloves that they used to mess around with when he was in first or second grade and said, "Now, I'm going to teach you for real," and they'd spar in the backyard and watch Tyson or Lennox Lewis on Pay-Per-View or old Mickey Ward fights because he was white and a scrappier fighter than all the rest and that's like you, you won't have the lunking muscle but you'll have the heart and as long as you stand your ground and never be afraid of your opponent you'll win. And then his dad would have a beer before work at the steamfitters and then he would come home later and miss dinner and say he had overtime, which was partially true, but partially he was drinking with his crew after the shift or when Burke was a sophomore his dad would reveal that sometimes it would be the titty bar but don't tell your mom and a little later that year because he was so loaded he forgot where he parked his car and his dad and his buddies downstairs for poker night and then his dad getting a DUI after a beef and beer for an old high school friend and somewhere in there Burke stopped caring as much in school because his dad seemed happy enough and never really got too overjoyed at his grades anyways and his dad saying half of it was bullshit that they taught him in there and Burke appalled that his dad had waited so long to tell him that and then they started drinking together on the back porch and his dad lit a cigarette and Burke with his jaw on the floor because his dad didn't smoke and his dad saying he had quit the day he was born but now I'm almost fifty and you're almost out of the house and fuck it we don't live forever anyway and then one day in late August his dad helped him move into the dorm and slipping him a sticky note with an address and saying, "You'll be getting beer anyway, I figured that is better than asking some North Philly bum," and a week later Burke, McNamara, Dempsey, and Sherdian each posing for their fake I.D.'s and each of his buddies saying his dad was the greatest.

It may have been better to let it all crumble away and see what remained. It may have been better to be that fake name, Eric Floyd, on that I.D. who lived on the made up street in a made up town, well not made up, but far enough away from this life. Better than to be stuck between the boy that had the bright future who was squandering his talent with each waking day not nose-deep in a book and the Burke who realized finally one day that he was a Burke and whose dad was so cool and he was cool for letting that talent float away and people saw his long hair and classic rock t-shirt and cigarette hanging from his lip and had him figured out. So you might as well get wasted and listen to good music and exhale that cigarette for a moment too long because that tension is leaving your body, and if someone says something to you or looks at you funny just punch them in the face because one day it'll come crashing down on you anyway and you'll probably be alone but today your boys are with you and they have your back and they want you to take them to high places but if you fall off the cliff they'll be there too and not say a word because you have some charisma and people think you're funny and even repeat your expressions and so they were in Harrington's and Sheridan bought a round of Jameson and they all slugged it down.

Oh and Sheridan, that magnificent man, the embodiment of what they all, combined, could be. Statuesque and handsome like a Ralph Lauren model with not a single hair out of place, bluntly refusing to grow his hair just because now he finally could. He with the flittering obsessions that seemed to run away with the seasons. Adroit in all it seemed: music, art, literature, and mathematics. He especially scoffed at all of the tales of drunken brawls at Temple frat houses, for he could perform a simple Jiu-Jitsu submission hold and even a D-1 athlete would be gasping for air like a minnow on the dock not even worthy enough to be used for crab traps at the bottom of the ocean. He remained steely as much as possible, but the early drinking had started to loosen the bolts on his otherwise titanium silo of a human personae. And it was becoming more evident in his mind that it was such a personae. He was marveled at by women, here at Harrington's even, three big-breasted girls in white, green, and orange tank tops could not take their eyes off him, and he had his share in his short life, but it was a facade. Not gay, but sexually ambivalent, as he seemed to be, ambivalent that is, about most things. Maybe it was the instant precision, that lack of a struggle that made it all interesting. Why obsess over women or sex when it was so automatic? Why play music forever once you get the gist of it? When you reach mastery and you'd rather not spend your weekends like these pathetic dipshits playing "Whiskey in the Jar" in a fake Irish accent to a crowd that's not even listening to you? He almost felt the same way about drinking, and to an extent, hanging out with his friends in general. The effect of drinking was fine, and he liked when it made him feel mellow, but the taste was nearly painful, and most drinks tasted like chilled, stale piss. So, to counter this apathy, he'd order the shots early in the night, or day in this instance, because there was at least more spectacle to it. More tension in seeing the glasses lined up, let the people either grimacing and sucking in air and making their cheeks all puffy in excitement and anticipation of the intense kick of the hard liquor and the spiral into drunken madness that would follow. He, of course, also appreciated this immediate high. This act, and he being known as the "partier" or "wild man" also suited his lack of real connection with these friends. In all the years they had known each other, he could only count a handful of meaningful conversations he had with them. They'd talk and he'd be two steps ahead of them, and he'd grow bored, or he'd bring up a topic out of their range of comprehension and easily give up. It was better to yell things out a window, or hoot and clap his hands, and shake his fist to a song and spot some chicks than to drop this whole thing and just go home and focus on the next project.

After a while at Harrington's, the four grew tired of the constant pushing and shoving that comes with a large crowd, especially a crowd that grew more sloppy and belligerent by the minute, so they ventured down Frankford Avenue a few blocks to Tom's Sportsmans Pub, a place out of the way and lowly enough to surely not be crowded. As he left the dim barroom of Harrington's, Dempsey felt disoriented by the bright sun and realized it was only two PM. Masses of green plodded up and down the streets of Mayfair, filling the air with drunken slurs and empty threats and laughter as school bus after school bus drove by, with even more shouting and hollering. Dempsey was in the stage of drunkenness where he would be highly irritable. He wanted to turn and set straight any buffoon who would stumble into him or turn his shoulder, but he fought the urge and kept walking. Too much trouble lately. Too much finger wagging by his mom or dad as he stumbled in late or showed up with a welt on his face from a fight, or the girls who scurried out of his room and out the back door as his parents arose. His fantasy returned to his mind: he and his three boys living in a house together, drinking nearly every night and doing as they'd please--this, the realistic fantasy. He studying for nursing school and then becoming a nurse and making decent money and not really worrying about anything else. Yet, he also had that grandiose fantasy of some fame or riches and renown and having a lovely wife or even he and his boys in some mansion of a house, and the money just coming in and no one worrying about work or anything of the sort. Just a fantastic dream with no real means of achieving it. Some wild scenario, a magic lamp with a million wishes.

They arrived at Tom's Sportsmans and began playing darts. Dempsey played Sheridan while Burke and McNamara smoked outside. Sheridan, of course, was skilled at darts as well, and was a challenging opponent for Dempsey, who was a decent player himself. Playing cricket, Dempsey was reliable to hit at least one number between 15 and 20 on one of his throws, mainly single scores, whereas Sheridan would hit doubles or triples and take an early lead. Sheridan was a pitcher in high school, and his precision showed at this game. However, with the early lead, Dempsey eventually caught up and the two were tied with only bullseye left. That was the great equalizer. Even a precise thrower like Sheridan fell to its torments--forcing him to hold the dart slightly differently each time, adjusting his stance, and arch his elbow. Dempsey hit the green circle for one; Sheridan followed with one of his own. Then, each fell into a dry spell of about eight throws until Sheridan, on a rope, threw straight into the red eye of the board and won. Dempsey bought him a beer.

She felt the layer of makeup on her face on her face, worried it was dissolving with the sweat of the day. She was now at her fifth bar of the afternoon. It was a fun enough day to start, but her friend Rebecca bumped into her old boyfriend, Dave, a loser wannabe pot dealer, and they went back to his apartment to fuck. Ann stayed around for a little while, but then she started to dance with some guy in a "Kiss Me I'm Shitfaced" t-shirt and Polo hat and she was gone too. Jane was still with her here at Tom's, but she was a lightweight going in and out of consciousness next to her at the bar. Even she was getting hit on with her eyes barely open. She just wasn't as pretty as her friends, Fauna surmised. She was pretty enough as a little girl, with pigtails and gingham dresses, and every Sunday her mom and dad would go to church at Saint Timothy's and then have breakfast at Mayfair Diner, and her dad, even though he was a gruff, six foot four construction worker, he would play Barbies with her and put that little doll in her pink convertible and say in his best feminine voice, "Let's Go Shopping," and put a little sun hat on her and even comb her hair. Then, one night when he was working on repaving a stretch of I-95, a drunk driver clipped him and his body went flying into a concrete barrier and he was dead. He was so big and tough she never thought in a million years he had the capability of dying. And then, about four years later, her mother remarried to Joe, who had two older boys,

Ron and Eric, and then moved into a three bedroom row home in Tacony, and he and her mom would never be home at nights as Joe was a truck driver for Tasty-Kake and her mom was a nurse at Nazareth Hospital. So Ron and Eric would get fucked up on beer or weed or sometimes pills and have their scummy friends over and those friends would always hit on her and one groped her when she was thirteen and they were about sixteen to eighteen and even Ron tried some shit on her one time, but they were always around and eventually she started fucking their friends and it made her feel like a grown woman and a woman who was wanted. But then she started really partying with them and she started to gain weight and get acne and those friends didn't seem to care as much about her, and they would still fuck her, but they didn't make any overtures or try to sweet talk her and they'd just take her upstairs and do what they had to do. Then she would stare in the mirror for hours and wonder why God was so cruel to plague her face with these oily, red and white pustules and she'd have to strategically place the right hues of makeup on her cheeks and nose and forehead and try to not look like some clown putting paint on bumps and everyone thinking she was trashy and just a whore who wanted it, and she was, but so was everyone else, but those girls could just sit there and wait for those dogs with their tongues wagging to approach them and try to spit game and suddenly become hack poets and then if they said yes they could just lie there and let that dog do all of the work, whereas she would have to do the work and do the dirty and memorable things to make up for this makeup whore and then they still wouldn't call her back.

So here she was at this shitty bar and there were some old fogies, but also a group of four young guys, probably not even old enough to be there, and probably at least one of them would want to jump onto here like a rabbit and then hop away and put another notch on their rabbit belt. And that rabbit ended up being Dempsey and they did it in the alley behind Tom's like stray cats and she took him to her house in Tacony and they did it again, and he hung around and had some beers with her and she at least felt temporarily wanted. But then her step brother Ron came home drunk from the Shamrock Shuttle too and started to give Dempsey some shit until Fauna interceded and ran up to her room with Dempsey and him sitting on the mattress on the floor and thinking how bare it all was, just a bed and a mirror and a few photobooth pictures from some wedding she attended and they were about to hook up again when they heard a loud bang on the door and they watched from her window Ron step outside and begin yelling and pointing his finger at two guys in their mid-twenties, and the guys kept barking, "Where's our money," and then the one guy grabbed Ron by the collar and headbutted him and Ron collapsed to the sidewalk and the guys rummaged through his pockets and finding nothing and then stormed into the house. Fauna suddenly gained courage and slammed open her door, half-clothed, and rushed down the steps to confront the two intruders.

"Get out of my fuckin' house, scumbags. Leave my family alone," Fauna screamed in the living room.

"Ronnie owes us four grand. Reno ain't givin' him anymore chances."

"Well he don't have it. Get the fuck out!"

The one with a goatee then took out a knife.

"You better give us every dime in the house, or this is the last time you see your brother or your boyfriend here alive."

"Fuckin' scum. I have two hundred bucks in my room."

"Jewelry too sweet Fauna."

"Fuck you."

As she went up for the money, he pointed the knife towards Dempsey, and Dempsey gave him the fifty dollars in his wallet.

Dempsey walked home through the Tacony Industrial Park. Warehouse after abandoned warehouse, crumbling sidewalks and driveways sandwiched between I-95 and the Delaware River. The Tacony Palmyra drawbridge was up, as a cargo ship passed through and the cars were temporarily trapped in Philadelphia. For as far as he could see, it was nothing but rubble; a dream lost and fading with each day. Ghosts in a tomb world with no foreseeable way out. The liberty was a lie. Brotherly love was some obscene joke. All he thought about was making his way home and to leave as soon as possible. It was night, and the party was over.

And so Fauna sat in the living room with her step brother who was holding a package of frozen spinach to his jaw and speaking only in epithet and obscenities, and she knowing she would never see that handsome curly blonde haired boy again. Then she'd be just another story he'd tell his boys about and he'd describe tonight and it'd probably be the most exciting thing to ever happen to him, but this was her fucking life, and he'd just go back to college on Monday and think about that white trash girl in the white trash house and he'd ace his exams and have some model life and she'd always be in some dingy bar drinking on a random Tuesday because she'd never have some 9-5 Monday to Friday job and the department store or restaurant only told her her days two days in advance and her "weekends" would be days when no one else would have off or feel like having a few drinks, so she'd just fall into degenerates like Ron, and she'd probably get knocked up at some point to one of these losers and she'd keep spinning and spinning until the day she'd say she had enough and find the college applications, but she'd look at her high school transcripts and GPA and get discouraged and lose that thought for a while and then she'd see the hours needed for a degree and the price, and she'd say no again, and then one day she'd work her way all the way up to the admittance essay and she'd cry at her desk becuase she could not think of one positive trait about herself and she'd slam the laptop shut and never think of it as a reality again and so she just went into her room and stared at the phone until the pill Ron gave her set in and she shut her eyes to go to sleep.

CHAPTER FOURTEEN

Dempsey coughed as he went into the fridge to get a beer. It was a wet, mucousy kind of cough that continued until it got raw and dry and Dempsey felt momentarily like he could not breathe. He figured it must have been either the drop in temperature on this November day or something he caught at Crozer Hospital. No, he wasn't a nurse, but a nurse's aide at the hospital in Chester, PA. He did not fare all that well in college and was unable to be accepted in a city nursing program after completing his associates, so he dropped out for about two years, working odd jobs here and there, until he was able to return to a job in health and almost simultaneously go back to school for public health. By now, of course, Burke and McNamara had graduated, but he still felt vindicated that he had finally made it on Temple's campus. Plus, he was now finally living on his own with Burke and McNamara in Mayfair, a block away from Frankford and Cottman. Harrington's Pub a stone's throw away.

Although it had been etched in his mind to move out of his parents' house since he graduated from Judge, it was still fairly hard to leave when the day finally came. His dad, still hobbling after his string of back injuries, insisted on helping him lift boxes and furniture into the U-Haul, and then, when his dad had to concede and admit the pain, sitting in a lawn chair dictating to Connor and his brothers the best way to stack everything to utilize every square inch of space. Kevin was unbelievably a junior at Bloomsburg University, and John a freshman at La Salle. Kevin was a moderate partier up in school, but he maintained strong grades and was on his way to a degree in education. John was in business and taking prerequisites for the time being, and had hopes of starting his own landscaping business. Connor and his brothers would work with their father for Mercer Lawn Care on occasion moving lawns and spraying pesticide on residential house and business parks in the suburbs. It was always on the side for Connor and Kevin, but John took a real interest to the work. John figured since Mercer focused on the larger development, he could service the door to door row home in Holmesburg. Always a pragmatist. A young man uncomfortable if he wasn't working or moving around in some capacity, even as he helped Connor to move, a smile never entered his face, no jokes or moments of slack. If anything, he would be uneasy during the moments of reprieve, and he would revert to innocuous talk about the Eagles or some other sports news. Connor, especially on the day he was finally leaving, wondered if that's all it would ever be. Would they ever really get a brother-to-brother conversation. Would Kevin ever belt out some glimpse of his soul? He received it ad nauseam with John, but Kevin had almost a fear for conversation. To Connor, it was some deep fear of failure, of some immense reverence for the word that if he got one or few of them wrong they would be out there and each word would be etched in everyone's mind for eternity. It was irrational and over-analytical, as everything was with Kevin, but in a way, his lack of speaking actually made it somewhat of a self-fulfilling prophecy for when he did converse, everyone certainly took notice. And, with his want for perfection in his words, he would stutter or correct his words mid-sentence, and it would all be rhythmically jarring and John would be embarrassed and get back to some work or wring his hands or take out his phone and act busy. Maybe Connor could have done something differently. Maybe he could have went for that meaningful conversation, no matter how awkward, until it finally came out. Well, it probably never will now, he thought as the last of the boxes were in the U-Haul and he stepped into the vehicle.

Connor looked at that old row home and it suddenly felt like it was no longer his. Not longer his house, but his parents' house. His mom and dad walked to the Ford 150 and Kevin and John went into his Relient K. His mom was against the idea of moving in with McNamara and Burke as he had little to no money, and she thought they were bad influences on him at times, but as he knew she would, she softened and moving day brought a tray of hoagies from Marinucci's and was running around with ice-cold bottles of water for everyone. Then, with the last box unloaded, he filled the U-Haul with a quarter tank of gas, returned it and drove with McNamara and Burke, his boys, into his new home.

Dempsey returned to the living room with a beer for himself and one for Jenna, a nurse from work at Crozer whom he had been dating for about a month, and sat down on the couch next to her. She was a thin, attractive blonde from Wilmington who was, without hyperbole, some type of miracle of a human being. Other nurses would complain about patients as soon as they left the room, only to plaster on the fake smile again when that poor creature pressed the little red button or it was time for some cafeteria mush or time to take vitals. However, Jenna never complained once, even when she had every right to. She would not even disparage other coworkers or administrators. She especially treated Dempsey, and all other aides, with genuine appreciation and kindness; he would be lucky to get eye contact or a "thanks" from most staff. Not only would she never complain, she would do absolutely anything to make a person's day, be it a kind remark, a joke, or just taking five minutes to listen to a coworker or patient unload their grief on her, and somehow not feel burdened or fatigued in the process. This relationship was young, certainly, but Dempsey had a flood of feelings which he hadn't experienced in some time. She listened attentively, looking into his eyes with this wonderment, her hazel, nearly green eyes glassy and shimmering like a freshly polished champagne flute, her mouth expressive with each word he spoke, little lines from her nostrils cresting and rippling out to her fine cheek bones and the fantastic swell of white which was her smile, nearly bright enough that he feared what would happen if he stared at it face on. Her tiny mannerisms and signs of caring, fussing over his comfort when he sat in her apartment to watch a movie, scampering to the kitchen to grab him a drink when she noticed his glass was empty, sliding him an extra pillow when she noticed him craning his neck slightly, even as he insisted he was fine but nonetheless grateful for the gesture anyway. She was a nurse, sure, and some of it was just in her blood, but Dempsey believed that she was starting to develop some love for him. This would be a true test for her today: withstanding a football Sunday at Dempsey, Burke, and McNamara's house. Burke would start drinking the moment he woke up, which was about seven AM, make his bets and set his lineups, and then plop a seat on the La-Z-Boy. He was now a steamfitter like his dad, and it was ingrained in him to wake up at the break of dawn, no matter how hungover he may have been. His hair was also now all gone, though his habit of smoking had not. If anything, it was steadily increasing to nearly two packs a day, which he smoked in the house. The cigarette smoke, compounded with McNamara and if they had any other guests over, bothered Dempsey, and made him cough and wheeze, but these were his boys, and they deserved the dream realized of smoking on a La-Z-Boy or a couch, and not outside in the freezing cold missing the game. Dempsey looked at Jenna frequently to see if the smoke bothered her, but she didn't whine in the slightest. If anything, Dempsey was the one to almost force them to cut back, as it was becoming increasingly harder for him to breathe with the cough that he was fighting through.

After a particularly noisy and painful coughing spell, Dempsey took a swig of beer and watched the game next to Jenna. As he coughed, she would gently place her hand on his back and gaze at him in concern. She was not a huge sports fan, but she seemed to tolerate the incessant statistic talk or player debates amongst the boys. Jenna did not sit there clearly utterly bored, but looked from speaker to speaker and the TV, eager to learn like the teacher's pet sitting in the front of the room, hands crossed on the desk and eyes glued to the teacher. She even laughed along when Burke made his often ridiculous, obscene comments, or did his little hip wiggle whenever the Eagles, or one of his fantasy football players succeeded. She's truly great, Dempsey thought, and I need to be good if I want to keep her. He had lived in the revelry of being a bachelor, to put it mildly, but she was this pure-hearted spirit that he knew he could not lose. He had to suppress those hound dog tendencies--it was time God-damnit. One step at a time. Treat her right, be faithful, put her first. I'll still live with Burke and McNamara here, but maybe one day propose, get married, maybe have kids. He stopped the thought as best he could. He was getting ahead of himself. McNamara lit another cigarette and Dempsey could only think about getting this irritation out of his lungs. It was bad. He knew health. He was aware of the symptoms, but he was twenty-six and he was young, and it was just some virus some patient passed along to him, part of the job, always being a little sick. Dempsey leaned back in his chair and took another swig of beer. This in front of him is all that he had wanted, It was foolish to think of the future, both positive and negative. And hey, if the Eagles win, everything is that much better.

CHAPTER FIFTEEN

The kitchen wallpaper was patterned with yellow marigolds in a blue vase. She put the paper up when they first moved into the house, nearly thirty years ago, and the once brilliant white in between the marigolds was now nearly brown, a product of time, obviously, and her mother coming over and smoking cigarette after cigarette, even though it still made Tara cough and the boys would complain about the smell, a smell that would not go away for nearly a week. Time when the boys flinging food on bad days when they were stubborn eaters and slapped the food from their plates and whined and cried until she took the food away and picked them out of their high chairs and placed them in front of the TV. Time when food was flung on good days when they would help her bake Christmas cookies or she would turn the lights off and place the birthday cake from Acme in front of the birthday boy with the frosting message and the boys' favorite characters, be it Batman, Ninja Turtles, Power Rangers, or Bert and Ernie. She had been meaning to take the wallpaper down years ago, but she never got around to it. Just when she would resolve herself to do it, one of the boys would have homework or a project she needed to help them with, or they would need a ride to, or get picked up from, practice and then she would remember they needed groceries and then the rugs looked like they needed to be vacuumed and it just never got done. She cringed at what people entering the home might think, and these days she would get more and more anxious about having people over, even if it was Connor, Kevin, or John's friends. She would think they all thought her house was representative of poor white trash, having thirty-year-old wallpaper for Christ's sake. She would try to tell herself it didn't matter, but deep down she knew it did. Even now, as Connor sat across from her with his girlfriend and broke the news that he had cancer, lymphoma, she could only think about the wallpaper. Of course, she should have been thinking about her son, and she felt guilty that she hadn't and knew this was because it was too hard to truly think about right now. She could even step back from the whole devastating news and think of the miserable tableau of her at the kitchen table staring off at the petals of the marigolds while Jenna's face was flooded with tears and Connor studied his hands and then darted his eyes in all directions nervously, that these reactions were all very typical and natural when dealing with a serious diagnosis and many people consciously or subconsciously taking measures to avoid this heavy emotion and thinking of anything but the matter at hand. She had seen it a million times over her years of being a nurse, and she feared that the true emotion would never come--that Connor would be like any patient, that her knowledge and experience with death had truly numbed her at this point. Though, she knew there was something she had to say. Would it even matter? Everyone at the table was a nurse as well to some degree. They knew the lines. They knew the "There are great treatment options. X amount of people survive this type of cancer, and you are young and in good shape. This doctor is fantastic...The support of family and friends is crucial...You are a fighter and we will beat this thing together." It was all so ubiquitous it was basically useless in saying, so she took a sip of coffee and said, "God always has a plan," which may have been worse than anything else and she could see in his eyes it angered him, but it was the only thing in her heart at the moment and she looked down and took his hand and fiddled with the scapular on her neck.

"Do you think we should tell Dad and Kevin and John," Connor asked in a quiet, shaky voice.

"It's up to you. Whenever you feel comfortable," Tara responded, drawing more courage through those years of saying something similar, and now reflexively stuck to her were these comforting words and soft tone.

"Okay. I'm ready to tell them," he said and squeezed Jenna's hand. His mom returned a moment later with his dad and brothers. The look on their faces already etching deeply into his soul to be the picture that always permeates in the mind, the stray leaves in the pool that you can somehow never expel. They all with their eyes wide and trying not to breathe heavily. His dad begrudgingly walking with his cane, his two brothers looking strong and stout--truly men, all of them walking into an ambush; Connor getting them all together by just saying he wanted to catch up with everyone and for them to meet his girlfriend Jenna, when in reality it was this. This cruelty that the oncologist delivered to him with such ease. This cruelty that led nurses and doctors to tilt their necks and place their hands lovingly on his shoulder, saying, "You better get checked out," and he putting it off and putting it off until he almost passed out on the staircase because he could not breathe. Now, they knowing through intuition that what he would tell them would be bad and they would get upset and confused or even angry or not really having much of a reaction like his mom, and then he sucked in his breath and just said, "I have cancer."

His dad bit his lip and absent-mindedly asked, "How bad is it? Did you catch it early?"

"It's attacking my lymphatic system and seems to be moving into my heart and lungs," he responded and all three men before him clenched their fists and turned away. His dad took a step to the railing where Connor's old Crispin baseball hat still hung on a metal rung. That little blonde boy with his big Rec Specs who could barely hit the ball off the tee, and then got the hang of catching the ball and not looking away in fear. Those cold nights in early March cheering him on behind the chain-link fence at Pollock or Thomas Holme Playground, and Connor waving to him from third base with a huge smile on his face because he worked on his grounders and graduated from the outfield to infield, and the hot corner, no less, and soon enough he no longer even needed to wear those Rec Specs and he hit a homerun one April night, and all his dad could see was this fighter motoring around all of the bases and beating the ball to home plate and getting the game ball at the end and having all of his friends on the team sign it and then getting large Slurpees at 7-Eleven and Connor talking about it for a week straight. It all seemed like a moment ago, and now was he going to be taken away? For the first time in months, Connor's dad, Michael Dempsey, no longer felt the pain in his back, though he would have traded those aches for anything else than this.

Kevin and John began to cry and hugged Connor. He seemed so unbreakable--he was their idol: tough, handsome, smart, and cool. Everyone knew them from Connor. "Oh, you're Dempsey's brother? Dempsey is the man! Tell Connor..." It was some bad joke. That's all it was. Damn, Connor was strong enough to beat it anyway.

"What happens now?" Kevin asked once the tears subsided.

"Chemo in about a week. I need to stop work and school. Just want to survive at this point."

"You got it man. You'll be fine. I love you, man," John blurted out and then burst into tears once again. His sopping wet face then landed on Connor's shoulder as he hugged him. It was years of emotion finally released.

Connor called Burke, who was the first person he told after Jenna, and asked him to invite all of their friends over to his parents' house to break the news. It would be a party of sorts, as everything seemed to be. A wake while he was still alive. It was hard to think of, the idea that he might die. Before even telling anyone, he anticipated their reactions. They would talk in the affirmative. "You got this, man. Kick cancer's ass," and so forth. He would move on from the conversation. He knew they wouldn't pry too much into the specifics of his condition, but he somewhat wished they would. It was not a good diagnosis, and there was a strong possibility that he would die. Should he tell them this? Did they deserve to know? Did he even want to know? You live your whole life trying to be as strong as possible. To be tough and the victor in the fight, and to live teetering on reckless abandon where you take shot after shot and stay up 'til the sunrise with your boys, while still understand you have a duty to make something of your life, to have a career that contributes positively to society while also hitting some personal goals, maybe for yourself, but more selfishly so you don't seem like a buffoon when you are introduced to strangers, "Oh, you're not a college graduate. Oh, you are just a nurse's aide. Do you have any hobbies? Do you play an instrument or arts and crafts or cook or have a rigorous workout routine? Oh no, then what do you do? Watch superhero movies and sports and ref basketball games from time to time and drink more beer than you should and sit in your apartment while your two friends smoke like chimneys and they're perfectly fine and you're the one with cancer like a dope."

He had yet to truly consider this possibility; this death. He felt himself barely out of the embryonic state. A human not close to being formed, and now bracing for the reality of nonexistence. It was not something he wanted to think of fully. The twist of fate so far was clearly not in his favor, so why dwell on the probabilities and likelihoods. It was not fair, though nothing was, so it would happen when it would happen. Yet, he could feel the brevity of it all, and felt that he needed to move quickly. It was a sign as bright as the sun. A sign that this could all end soon. You might not get eighty years. You will most likely be lucky if you get a handful. Go out and get the ring for Jenna tomorrow. To hell with it being too soon. Book the trip to Florida, and Dublin, and anywhere else. Write. Just write it down. It doesn't need to be some masterwork novel, just some proof that your were here and you had a thought or two before you left. Do not go away quietly. Do not be the withered corpse in the hospital gown. If it'll get you, it'll have to find you.

Burke, McNamara, Sheridan, and about ten others showed up to Connor's parents' house, and he told them. They said things to him as he expected them too, and oddly brought up people they knew that also had cancer and survived. He figured people had to make sense of it; that there had to be a comparison, another case study. People are incredible, he concluded, even if their words are jumbled and awkward and it irritates you slightly. They care and they want to show they care. They cannot accept suffering, it ultimately is an impossibility. There needs to be a horizon through the dim haze. Pain cannot be tolerated if it causes further pain. Look, they even continue to drink and laugh and bring up comical anecdotes until they've forgotten it all too, and soon I'll be out of their minds too, because that's how it has to be.

After everyone left, he kissed his mother goodbye and shook his father and his brothers' hands, and they returned to Jenna's apartment. While she slept, he took one of her rings out of her jewelry box, traced it onto a Post-It, and went to sleep, worn but his mind racing.

CHAPTER SIXTEEN

He found himself most of the time staying in bed after chemotherapy treatment, either at his parents' when he was feeling particularly weak, or at his apartment when his strength was there. It had been nearly a month since the diagnosis, and he was feeling relatively good. He was tired, sure, and his hair was gone, but he didn't feel like a man about to die. In fact, he was often tempted to head downstairs or up the block to Harrington's to have some beers like before. It would be fine to have a few, but he also didn't want to jinx it. His body was responding well to the treatments, and the sobriety seemed to bring a clarity to his mind which he hadn't possessed in some time. He felt idea after idea rush into his head, plot after plot, character after character, but he would get too excited or overthink it in his mind and it vanished. Was the fiction even worth it at this time? He loved superheroes and comics, and he wished he could create a character that would be compelling, memorable, and a world and serious plot that could endure. However, this never came to fruition when he placed pen to paper. He kept returning to reality. The world was not filled with Spider-Men or Iron-Men swooping down and saving the day. Nor was it inhabited by Green Goblins or Doctor Dooms. It was the vagueries that were truly terrifying and compelling in his mind. The gray area where opposing forces or ideologies lived and stirred for eternity. This was where cancer grew. This was the impossibility of the $A + B = C$. An effect with no clear causes, and maybe not $A + B$, but the whole damn alphabet and even some hieroglyphics for good measure. When the equation cannot be solved, and we are stuck between wonderment and frustration. He could peruse book after book on this subject, this cancer, but in the wide variety of causes, they all may have just said it was life that caused it. A mutation that occurs one day. One cell becoming two, and suddenly there are way more than are needed. He pictured these growths building and building, his body teeming with unwanted matter until they took up every inch and there was no room left for his heart or lungs and then of course his brain and all of these wonderful little unwritten stories would be one with the mud and maybe some grass or a fantastic tree or flower would grow from that mud and a tiny cell of him would be in that bark, way down deep, and he'd feel a robin land on the branch on a May afternoon, chirp and sing its little heart out, and then indifferently pluck off a twig and fly away to its nest. So he thought of Burke and Sherdian and Jenna and his family, and he thought of them as characters and how he could write in a raw and authentic way, but then they might read it and see one negative characteristic and be fixated on that characteristic for eternity or feel even more betrayed because the character did not fit him or her at all, and he or she would feel like the entire relationship was at best misinterpreted and at worst a sham. So he just went on his phone and scrolled through news feeds or played games and the day was soon gone. If not this writing, what can there be? Sometimes this thought strained him, and kept him in this perpetual limbo. The cliches of living each day as if it were your last permeated in him, for it could very well be true. Better to live in no worry, or to make some final impact?

It was nearly five PM on a Friday, and soon Burke and McNamara would be getting home from work. Burke, from converting an old Tacony factory into a charter school, and McNamara from his graduate internship program at La Salle. Both of them most likely somewhat envious that Connor needed to stay home while he recovered. That was fine in the present, but this also meant a day when he could not earn money to pay for his enormous treatment costs. And then that specter of death returned to his mind and flooded each crevice in his skull with the black sludge and demonish, electric banshees bolting from wall to wall of his psyche and howling and speaking in tongues and demons cackling and laughing and the grand tormentor rising above them all and casting two lighthouse beams of blood red until all he could see was this fluorescent red and he was consumed. He flailed like an infant in the ether and then the illumination softened and the backdrop dulled to a wool gray and all of the words were before him as in a golden scroll and the pen larger than him dangled before his outstretched hands, but lo it was too heavy to render, so he jostled past it and touched the scroll, only to have it dissolve into sand. The sand forming a perfect diamond and the bags beaming a radiant white. In the distance, he heard the ping of a metal bat against the leather ball, and this ping growing louder and myriad until it was a chorus singing this base-hit song in a-round and the crowd cheered and his father's face was before him, smiling so widely that the cheek muscles snapped with fatigue and his face grew dour and his father was soon in his La-Z-Boy with an ice pack on his back looking away and grimacing and grunting and stating, "I'm fine. I'm fine." And then the delirium ceased, and Connor was on the front step breathing in the cold because he had been indoors all day, and it was good to feel the true temperature, even if it stung his throat slightly and made him shiver.

Today was Burke's birthday, and they, as in Burke, McNamara, and Sheridan, discussed going to McFadden's downtown in Spring Garden. It was now they, and not he in the they, because the assumption was that he would not be coming-- that he was sick and weak and needed his rest like a typical cancer patient. It was not intentionally mean-spirited, but it was as if they were leaving him behind already, and it infuriated him.

Connor looked down the block; the one way, only wide enough for parking on one side, street. Snow fell down softly and flakes floated in the golden illumination of the street light until their suspension ceased and they tumbled to the sidewalk. A thin layer of frothy white was beginning to stick to car windshields, and some accumulation began to build on the wrought-iron railings and tin mailboxes of each row home. A small buildup, mostly a wet slush, soon appeared on the sidewalks. A pitbull and its owner walked by and boot and paw imprints were left as they passed. The night was a stark, yet brilliant black--almost glossy in its eternal velvet drapery of sky. Not a star to be seen, just the falling clumps of frost. He stayed still and allowed each drop to stay on his pale face, and even removed his cap so they could touch his smooth, bald head. In this moment, he swore he could not even hear the noises of the city, and if they were there, the tires screeching and sliding, the horns blaring, and the engines revving, it was only calm, ambient noise to him. This revelry could have been five seconds, or it could have been an hour, and it was of no consequence. The ploughmaster of time, the omnipresent driver of duty, reticent with the whip in his hand, brutal when you, the workhorses, stopped in fatigue, yet kissed you when the sun set and the work was complete and you begged for one more chance in the field, even if your back was sore and you neighed at every step, had this one time allowed Connor a reprieve. A bliss in the fragility of life. He, one with that snowflake having its moment of glory, that light all around before it lands on the earth and piled together with all of the rest. The meaning was not certain, and he had no way of fully articulating the joy in his bones. All he knew was that he would miss it when it was gone.

Burke and McNamara returned home from work, and Sheridan and his girlfriend Casey soon arrived as well, along with Casey's friends Shaina and Julie Lynn. Burke was filthy from a long day in and out of the cold of the steamfitters. His hands over the years were now calloused and layered in a thin film of black residue, and if you looked closely enough, you could see tiny burn marks from welding or soldering mishaps. He was "the man with the torch" as he liked to say, and an image of him pervaded with his dark, protective mask on and the steady, blue flame in his hand ready to sculpt and seal. An inferior storyteller would explain the job in a few short minutes, and brush it off as innocuous labor, but Burke could unravel a tale of a leaky pipe into a dire, life-or-death narrative, where, if not for Burke's bravery with the torch and skilled hand, hundreds of lives could have been lost. He was the constant hero, but not in a conceited way. It was just a true belief in himself that made him so captivating. McNamara and Sheridan, and Connor as well, may have been better looking to an extent, and may have possessed more diverse individual skills, but it was Burke they were all drawn to. It was he that three lovely young women, dressed up for a night in the city with their best jewelry, scarves, and mascara, could not take their eyes off of, even as he sat before them breathing smoke into their faces and covered in soot and grease.

Connor's friends and the girls sat in the living room drinking as Connor rested in his bed. It was time for dinner, but he had no appetite, yet he still had a pang in his stomach, to the point where a burning sensation would climb up his throat and it felt like he was going to vomit. He heard laughing and music below; the sweet sound of one of Burke's records warmly scratching a hippie album that was nearly forty years old. Jenna was working that night shift tonight, and she had promised to be over tomorrow in the early afternoon. He opened up the drawer of his nightstand and took out her engagement ring. When he bought it he had wanted to propose that day. He wanted that immediacy, that moment checked off of his abbreviated life--key events happening with the speed of a movie montage. Yet as he delayed that impulse, grimmer rationalizations entered his mind. Was it fair to marry her; to go through all of this, if he was just going to be gone soon? Didn't she deserve better than to be a widow at twenty eight? So he decided he needed to beat it first, this cancer. His treatments would last until the end of December, and then he would know. It was fitting that it could all be determined by the new year. A fresh start and all of that sentiment. He closed the ring case and placed it back into the drawer, under his undershirts and briefs. He would do it! He would beat it, he concluded and with a sudden spark of adrenaline, got up out of bed. Tonight he would join them. He would drink. Hell, he would even dance if the girls dragged him out there. This sickness would not win.

Connor was feeling content at McFadden's. It was good for him to have a beer in his hands and to be surrounded by people who were not sickly. His friends were slightly wary when he announced that he would be joining them, but after a few beers, they were now thrilled to have their buddy back. The thought of death was now gone, there was no way it could happen to Dempsey. He was too damn strong and tough for any such foolishness to occur; that was the consensus of he, his friends, and presumably everyone at McFadden's. He walked with a swagger unseen since their earliest days of drinking and entering bars. Dempsey was indestructible as he moved through the crowded bar, his head held high and without a trace of timidity compared to the typical person in such a crowded space. He would take on anyone and win. He was the alpha, indomitable male of his early twenties, the one that was not to be messed with because he was brave enough to do something about it. His bald head now made him that much more intimidating and severe, like a shaolin monk calm, but ready to strike if needed. Crowds even seemed to part before he reached them, as if he had telepathically told them to do so, and bartenders came to him in a moment's notice. Dempsey felt the eyes of women on him as he moved about the bar, and he generously returned such glances with his ice blue eyes, brooding and domineering simultaneously.

His friends were getting fairly wasted, and Burke in particular began to sway slightly and slur his words. Dempsey kept his drinking light, but was still feeling slightly fatigued due to his treatments. McNamara was trying to flirt with Shaina and Julie Lynn, though his flirting consisted of just going on at length about his job--which was not as easy to explain as say a nurse or steamfitter--so he felt the need to describe all of its nuances. McNamara's flaw was that he lacked that initiative, that striking calculation that came with true flirtation. He lulled them into a nice guy, not-really-flirting act, and then he would get frustrated when he would ask for a number or lean in for a kiss and the girl would not reciprocate. Dempsey decided to teach him how it was done, cut in the middle of McNamara and Shaina, and began flirting. Though he was not really that interested in the girl, and he loved Jenna, he was in the moment and began to fall back to old ways. Dempsey commented on Shaina's necklace, which was a silver chain with topaz chevrons of varying sizes, and said it went well with her brown eyes, and then proceeded to buy two jello shots from a waitress walking by. The two cheersed to Burke and Dempsey put his hand on the wall beside her as they talked. McNamara said he was going to get another beer, and the two were alone. Dempsey did not really want anything from her. Shaina was beautiful and had nearly perfect, round breasts, but he just wanted to see how far he could get her to go. Could he get her to fall over him for a kiss? Maybe say she wanted to sleep with him and he reveal he was in a relationship. Mainly just to see that he was still attractive to the world--bald, Chemo head and all.

She asked about the cancer because of course she knew, and as she asked, her face grew more delicate, almost to the point where Dempsey expected her to cry. He did not like this kind of sympathy because it brought him back to the thought of death, but then again, she said he was "so brave" and stroked his hairless head and he smiled like a puppy dog. She then asked him if he wanted to dance and they were on the dance floor.

The dance floor was pitch black except for the two white strobe lights and the rainbow light that spun around the room. Dempsey felt Shaina's body, and they soon locked hands as they moved to the DJ's pulsing beat, nearly no variation of a doo-dah doo-dah rhythm between songs. Shaina moved herself closer to him and he could feel her ass on his crotch wiggling side to side. He breathed heavily and continued moving his feet as best he could. She moved quickly, and he found it hard to catch his breath. The music pulsed in his ears until it felt like his eardrums popped and he could only hear a ringing. The strobing lights overwhelmed him, and it felt like he was underwater and drowning fast. He tried to suck in air, but there seemed to be nothing there. His hands were sweaty as well as his upper lip, a small rivulet flowing down the scar from his stitches. He could see Shaina locking eyes with him, and she placed her arms around his neck. He closed his eye--

CHAPTER SEVENTEEN

He did not even resemble the same person to her as she looked down on him sleeping in the hospital bed. He was bald, skinny, and so pale that she could nearly see through him. She had seen the look so many times that it seemed as common as looking at your alarm clock or the shower faucet or your underwear drawer. Yet, she only saw it when it came to her at the hospital, never the person prior. She never saw that true tragedy of illness, misfortune, and old age. That once was. That actual life. Connor was without those curly blonde locks, the muscular definition of his body, or the glow of weekends down the shore. She had all of the love and sympathy possible in her heart, but she also had the anger. The anger that her dad was taken by cancer, also lymphoma, when she was twelve. The anger of how the world treated her afterwards--family, friends, and teachers interacting with her as if she was made of tissue paper. Talking to her softly with wide eyes and bobbing their heads as if in tune with the hidden grief and devastation of each word she spoke. Hearing phrases like "I feel bad" or "My heart goes out..." more often than any person should. Falling hard for boys, then men, that required care and mending, only for them never to change and burn her in the end--at least they stayed who they were and didn't treat her like the poor victim. And then, meeting the strong guy, who was not perfect, but at least appreciated her and didn't define her by her tragedy, and he went and got sick and was a big enough idiot to go out partying with his friends at a bar downtown and send her speeding down I-95 to see him in the morning after working for twelve hours at night. Did he even care as much as she did whether he lived or died? Maybe that's how all of these men are built. If they're not out dying in wars or bashing their brains out in sports, then they're drinking themselves to death speeding down that road until they and machine are wrapped around the tree. The thought made her want to leave right then, but she could not. She would never be able to do so. How could she leave this young man, with cancer, to potentially die on his own? It would haunt her her entire life. People would sneer and talk behind her back. People would be shocked that such a kind, gentle nurse could do such a thing. "Oh, why I never–"

He talked about marriage often now. Why wouldn't he, she figured. She was good to him and his time may be running short. Why does the threat of death convince so many to live so? How often she'd listen to patients list the things they would do once they left the hospital room. How they would explore the world and try new hobbies and spend more time with family and friends and tell everyone how much they love them. She guessed this was the business that she was in--both nursing and with Connor. She kissed him on the cheek and straighten his blanket and sat in the chair beside him and waited for him to wake up and for her to finally sleep.

He spent seven days in the hospital, and it was not an experience he wanted to repeat anytime soon. It felt as if he was a display at a museum, in his hospital gown with an IV hooked to his arm and nurses taking his vitals and doctors examining clipboards and reminding him about overdoing it while in chemotherapy and his susceptibility for further illness if out and about in the world for too long. Worse than this though were the visits. Jenna being there was fine since she knew the environment and never fussed over him to the point of making him uncomfortable; however, the same could not be said about his mother who was constantly asking how he felt and if he needed anything and nearly had a panic attack any time he sighed or started to nod off. His dad essentially just sat there staring at the TV in the corner and seeming to do anything possible to not view his son in this position. Connor supposed it did not occur to anyone, himself included, just how dire this situation truly was. He was weak and the cancer was not diminishing. It was even suggested that a tumor was beginning to grow around his heart. There were potential options, such as radiation or proton therapy, but for now there was not much for him to do but sit there and hopefully get better.

He wanted to be alone most of the time, and shooed people away, even if they were persistent. After two straight days either in his room or sleeping in the waiting room, Connor finally convinced his mother to go home and get some rest. In a way, her persistence of staying just scared him more, for she had a genuine fear of leaving and something drastic happening. Even if it did , after two straight days, he needed some time to be by himself. He thought of extreme things, like drafting a will or writing a letter to each family member or friend, but it was better to just lie there and zone out on the television and medication. When hours passed, he did grow lonely, and regretted sending everyone away. He anticipated someone walking through the door at any moment, but eventually visiting hours were over and the idea left his mind. Jenna called to wish him a good night, and several friends texted him before he went to sleep.

By the sixth day, he was feeling better, though with not enough energy to do anything too strenuous. He was too exhausted to read, and the idea of writing seemed a hundred years away. His friends came to visit him every other day, all with this incredible look on their faces. A look that said, "This is really happening. Dempsey is really sick." Still, they all said just about the same things to him, "You got this man. You're tougher than this shit. You'll be fine and back out in no time." They were all doing what they could, and Dempsey appreciated how strong they were being for him. Surprisingly, it was McNamara who seemed to finally arrive to more realism as he visited him on this sixth day.

"I can't help but think this was my fault. Smoking and all that. Maybe I triggered this. Maybe you were more susceptible or something."

Dempsey looked out of the tiny window of his room in Penn hospital, seeing only brick and other wings of the building. This thought was certainly on his mind, but it would be worse, and not wholly accurate to agree with McNamara's conclusion, so he responded quite objectively, "It's not your fault. It's not Burke's fault. This is just an unfortunate thing that has happened to me, and I hate it because I don't want things to happen to me. I want to make things happen."

"You do, and you will. There's nothing like a comeback story," McNamara grinned, as they both had a love for story. McNamara even had a short story or two published in small online literary journals.

"I'll do my best to make that happen. If nothing, it's always interesting. You just start thinking about things, you know?"

"I can imagine..."

"Do you still believe you saw ghosts?"

"Oh jeez, ha ha I forgot about that. I really believed it at the time."

"Not anymore?"

"I guess I can't discredit what I saw, but you start to read stories and how your mind can play tricks on you. And I guess I'm older and I find it harder to believe in all of that, but I can't shake that feeling I had when it was all over."

"Peace?"

"Yeah, peace. An alleviation of worrying, you know?"

Dempsey nodded his head and looked about the room. All of these machines, medicines, and comforts designed to make him well.

"People keep telling me to fight, It just--"

"Happened to you."

"And it'll keep happening no matter what I do. Is it the struggle that I really want, or is it peace?"

McNamara thought for a moment. "How do you feel now?"

"I'm bored as hell."

"That might be your answer, man. Peace is some illusion--

some turn of phrase quote someone posted to their wall. You can only make a life, you can't just be in it. Rage!"

"Quoting Dylan Thomas for your anti-quote quote?"

"Ah, well I'm out here trying to make it."

They laughed and got off of the heavy conversation and discussed the projected Phillies' lineup. It was a good visit he had from his friend, and Dempsey began outlining potential characters for a potential story in his notebook.

He left Penn hospital after seven days and continued to recover at his Mayfair apartment for the rest of December. Doctors were able to target the growths around his heart and lungs, and the potential tumor was stopped for the time being. He was confident in survival, and he booked a surprise trip for him and Jenna to Disney World for Christmas to New Year's. He knew how obsessed Jenna was with Disney princesses and exactly at midnight of the New Year, Connor dropped to one knee and proposed to her in front of Magic Kingdom as fireworks exploded in the sky. She, of course, said yes.

CHAPTER EIGHTEEN

Two years later, and he went through two remissions and relapses, his wedding to Jenna, buying a house in Aston, and getting a little Shih Tzu named Bailey. He had been feeling strong as of later, a type of imperviousness of having to beat and get cancer again two times already, and most likely having to do it several more times before it was all said and done. He ran the 5Ks and attended the benefits whenever possible for cancer research. His hair had even grown back and there was optimism that he would be fertile once again. Jenna helped to get him a job at Crozer in the human resources department, and on Saturdays they would walk the Schuylkill River Trail or go to Kelly Drive to watch the regattas; often bringing Bailey as well. The idea of writing had passed from him slightly, though he still read nightly. If the writing was not coming he could at least read some of the greatest works possible, he reasoned. He'd spend nights when Jenna was working her night shifts on the couch with a thick book and Bailey on his lap in awe of the written word and enthused that each word was unlocking new capacities in his thought–undiscovered worlds hidden somewhere in the recesses of his mind. He saw Burke and the gang much less frequently, but when they did meet, it was like nothing changed. If anything, it was more enjoyable to laugh about their wild days and get caught up on the latest happenings. Sheridan and Casey were getting married in May, and Burke and McNamara did not want to jinx it, but they were happy with the girls they were currently dating. His mom and dad both recently retired, and they were saving up for a place somewhere close to Connor in Delaware County. His brother Kevin was working at a new charter school, the same one Burke helped to renovate, and seemed happy and supported. John was growing his landscaping business, called Dempsey Exteriors, which was booming as far as he knew. John had two Ford F-150s with his company logo and contact information decaled to the sides of the vehicle as well.

Yes, everything was going well, which made it that much more devastating when he was told the cancer had returned and a tumor was neatly wrapped around his heart.

He stepped out of Penn Hospital after the diagnosis, holding cancer and hospice pamphlets, cooled on the warm spring day by the shadow of the city. He drove around the streets of University City in his Toyota Corolla--the Relient was long gone-- a little lost but not caring to look up the directions on his GPS. This part of the city was clean and well maintained. Ancient buildings power-washed with care, three-hundred-year-old brick and mortar pristine maroon and beige colors, even nearly golden on some buildings. The streets were lined with zelkova and white birch trees in bloom and trimmed in a perfect roundness. College students strolled to class or conversed outside of cafes while joggers in tights and bikers wearing satchels meandered past them. A new, glass skyscraper shimmered in the sun, ripples of the Schuylkill River reflecting off the crystalline monolith. Traffic crawled along I-76, and the wail of car horns flooded the sky-- pointless yet cathartic.

He drove on down Girard Avenue, a Richter scale of progress and deterioration. Old storefronts abandoned and tagged with graffiti, to new city project buildings with even small patches of lawn in the front, new, trendy bars and a beer hall, the El, dim and foreboding as always, a piazza with new restaurants and a projector screen that televised world championship soccer matches on the old Schmidt Brewery building, a car wash with a row of cars extending into Orianna Street, its workers furiously shining hubcaps and windshields and drying any wet streaks from the extra-deluxe wash, kids popping wheelies down the block and cars double parked to pick up pizza orders, and finally the entrance to I-95 and the return home.

It had only been a year since he left the Northeast, but

it appeared so foreign. Bodegas and bars that once felt so cozy, now seemed threatening and of low standard. He thought fondly of his time living in Mayfair with Burke and McNamara, but his true home was Holmesburg. He passed Canstatter's, where they held Oktoberfest every year. Seeing it reminded him of holding that large beer stein, paying for food and drink with tickets, and hearing sprightly German music. A moment later he passed Thomas Holme Elementary and the playground, where he played baseball and basketball and had his first kiss on the jungle gym. He saw Out of Wack Jack's and Penny Gardens, where he shared many beautiful drunken nights with friends. Continuing on Holme Avenue, he saw Crispin Gardens Athletic Club, his "home turf" for baseball, and the old graves, one an obelisk said to be where Thomas Holme was buried, right next to Pennypack Woods, where he had his first sip of beer and ran from the police on many occasions. It was also where he fished with Burke and swung on a rope that hung over the creek, and it was all so easy and no one had to die.

He stopped his car at Pollock and walked over to the "A" where he and his friends spent many good nights and early mornings. The wax and grease still caked on to the sandstone to prevent wild kids from running up to the top--which proved ineffective as he and Sherdian, Burke, and McNamara ran up it that hazy morning prior to going to the Turkey Bowl. He wanted to climb up it once again, but he thought of bigger things. He looked over to the smokestack that stood above Pollock Elementary. It had always loomed there, like a watchful eye over the neighborhood. A tower of legend where a young boy climbed to his death and his body then incinerated by the internal combustion of this heat generator. A relic of a previous era, a former way, allowing the behemoth to cough out smoke throughout the years and trickle through the air. He feared it. He feared its height and the frailty of its rungs. He imagined taking a false step or a slick metal step betraying him, and his carnage on the roof or on the parking lot below, and the confusion his death would raise. Yet, he had thought of it his whole life. He thought of it as he walked home from school, mesmerized by the small, red blinking light at the top and the white plumes emanating from its mouth. He thought of it as he played pickup basketball at the playground or daydreamed during baseball games at third base. Yet he was tired of the events happening to him. Of the parents making the plans, of choosing the religion and the school to attend and the stiff collared uniform and sweater with the crucifix stitched over his heart; sick of the friends making the plans and choosing the music and who was cool and who was not, and sick of the cancer telling him his life was over and it was time to give in. He took a deep breath and coughed slightly as he exhaled and walked over to the wing of Pollock Elementary that was nearly level with the playground. He placed his hands on the metal bars of the window and propped himself up with the sill below. With firm footing, he continued to scale the metal bar window until he reached up to the lip of the roof, worked his feet up the bars, and with all the strength he had in his forearms, rolled himself up onto the roof of the school wing. Although it was a short climb, he was already fairly high up, as the lot for recess was about twenty-five feet below him. The roof was white and cracked along the edges. There were empty beer cans, cigarette butts, a hypodermic needle, about twelve tennis balls and five baseballs, three footballs, condoms, and even a tire spoke. The roof was also splattered with graffiti, mostly saying "PLK" and another tag that said "Zealot". He moved forward and casually kicked a Milwaukee's Best can off of the roof, not hearing the tin clang until three seconds later.

He reached the other half of the Pollock Elementary building, this end elevated about twelve feet because of the indoor gymnasium. Thankfully there was a ladder going up the wall, otherwise the climb would have been nearly impossible. He climbed the ladder gingerly until he reached the top and it was only the smokestack before him. It was made of nearly the same red and brown brick of his parents' house, yet covered in a coat of soot. He forced himself not to look out from this height, as he knew he would grow afraid and not continue. The height of the smokestack was longer than it appeared from the street, and from his acute angle, it nearly blotted out the sky. The metal rung was warm, and felt nearly soothing in his hand. He grabbed the next rung with his other hand and pulled up. His free hand trembled for a moment, and he could feel the wind pass through his fingertips until they gripped the next rung. His legs dangled against the brick until hesitantly they found the rungs below. He was fully on, and too late to come down now. Rung by rung he felt it, that cultivation of feelings flooding the senses--fear, triumph, rage, nostalgia, and joy--a grand kaleidoscope of sensation and experience. His hands burned, not from exhaustion or terror, but that a pursuit was now destination. He placed his hands on the brick ledge of the smokestack and pulled himself up. He looked down into the smokestack, smelling the burning embers and breathing in the heat. The vent was a metal grate, and he wondered if it was installed after the boy fell down it. In any case it gave him enough room to sit down. From the smokestack he was far above Ashton Road, and he could see the pools of Winchester Swim Club perfectly--drained but soon to be filled. He could see Holme Circle, and the full, actual circle and its tributary streets. He looked down on the blooming trees in Pennypack Woods, and even followed a hawk flying to its nest at a tree's highest branch. He wanted to see more--he was up here already, so he slowly stood up, the warm exhaust at his ankles and his feet on the edge. Here he was above it all. It was his home in full landscape--surveyed as Holme could not so many years before. This was the ink on that ancient papyrus brought to life. Whether Holme would have liked it or not, this is what it became. A pocket of the other dreamer, Penn's new Babylon. A pocket of middle class Irish Catholics who were flawed and hard to live with most of the time, but who were utterly brilliant in their love, even if it took a person a lifetime, or an abbreviated life to realize. And Connor turned to the other side of the stack, and saw the top of his parents', no, his still, roof. He knew their life had not been ideal, and that they deserved better than this tiny row home, but they were good people and they showed him love his entire life, and they would be bitter when the cancer finally killed him, but they shouldn't be because he was given a life that was truly sad to lose. He then outstretched his arms as if collecting all of Holmesburg within himself as the smoke began to climb up to his face and then pushed away by a soft breeze. He laughed to himself for a reason he could not explain and sat up there until he saw the sun set on his home.

CHAPTER NINETEEN

It could have been any day, his death that is. The treatment options were completely exhausted; the medications did not sedate the cancer, and the decision was made to take him off of all suppressants. The hospice team stopped by daily to check on him, and Jenna officially took a leave of absence from work. He just wanted to live his regular life at this point, in his home, with his wife and with his dog Bailey.

Being in the hospital could have prolonged things slightly, but it wasn't worth it if it meant being tied to tubes and being bathed like an infant with little to no senses remaining. Jenna was kind and loving as always, but he could tell she was also on edge. No matter how cliche, each moment was important. Each morning waking up alive, having a hearty breakfast (anything he wanted!), showering, walking Bailey with Jenna as they held hands, letting Bailey sniff every shrub or signpost she desired-- What was the rush anyway?--feeling the breeze on his face and the warm sidewalk against his sandals, watching a movie or show with Jenna on the couch, kissing her soft cheeks and making love to her on their bed, a soft down bedroom set her mother got for them for their wedding, eating a freshly made dinner Jenna prepared, along with a dessert, which they had in droves, and watching the NBA or NHL playoffs at night when it was just the two of them. And, they had their share of visitors. Jenna was fantastic at traffic controlling, sensing when he was getting tired and when company would be too much, and in tune to when he was feeling morose and needed to see his parents or brothers or friends. It was awkward and there didn't necessarily seem to be a right way of going about things, but he was as at peace with it all as well as could be expected. When people came, he mainly just wanted to learn more about them. There was so much to know about everyone, and it was tragic how much he didn't really know about say, his mom. What street did she grow up on? Was she popular? Who was her best friend growing up? He went through this interview process with each guest, and even wrote responses down in a notebook. Everyone was willing to abide, of course, but they also grew concerned with the level of exertion the questioning seemed to take and how furiously he would jot down the answers. These notes he would look at each night, as if studying for an exam on the central people of his life. Conversely, those guests wanted to talk about him. However, they did not want to know what he believed in, if he ever regretted anything, what he would do if he was healthy, even what he thought would happen after he was gone? All they wanted to talk about were past times, good old days, and occasionally tales of miraculous recoveries. These people meant well, and they were just trying to uplift his spirit, but he honestly just wanted truth--they owed him that much at least. He was going to die, and no amount of "hang in there buddys" and pats on the back were going to change that.

Connor still tried to write whenever possible. Some days with an overwhelming urgency that came with the sickness--the idea of living on through the word and leaving people with some trace of who he was. But the ideas were hard to come by, and it made him fatigued quite easily. He, in a way, often did not even want to go there, to spend those precious hours exploring what remained of his mind and body and leaving his soul on the paper. He figured he just wanted his life to have meaning, at least one piece of art or accomplishment that would be added to this world. He would just sit and stare at the empty pages, doodling with his pen and just hoping that the words would come, but they never did. He concluded that if he could not write when his time was at an end, it was never meant to be.

During his last few days, the coughing was incessant. He was offered medication to sedate him, but he refused--fearing a pill would knock him out and he would never return. He no longer had the strength to leave the bed, and he listlessly lied there watching TV and petting Bailey, who sat on his stomach. Jenna washed him up and asked if he wanted to see family and friends, and he said he did.

His mom, always strong, could not stop sobbing when she arrived. She saw it too often over the years--a person deteriorated and about to let go. His dad saw he was bad as well, but could not accept that his son was about to die. Tomorrow was simply always an option until it no longer was. His brothers said they would never forget him and that if they ever had kids, they would know about their Uncle Connor. Burke sniffled and held his hands to his face to hold back from crying. He said he would quit smoking and Connor told him he would always have his back. McNamara and Sheridan were set to visit the following morning, but that night, Connor rolled over, kissed Jenna, and said, "This is it," and took his final breath.

*

A fantastic bright consumed him and he was utterly weightless. Without body, without pain, he was just consciousness. All mysteries were revealed in him. All that was to be known and unknown. He was in eternal water. Wave after wave flowing through him. Alone, but feeling all. He was with Jenna, who was sobbing into tissue after tissue over him. With Bailey, who walked around confused and yelped as the body was carried away. Bailey loved him, and he could now understand her. It was odd viewing his body being incinerated, but that was his wish-- to utterly destroy every speck of cancer within him. Jenna would place his urn on the mantel, though he wished he could tell her to just send it out with the breeze--but she would know all of that one day. She would dwell on his memory for years, and wait nearly twenty years to seriously date someone again. He was grateful for her devotion to him, but he knew she would miss out on the joy of love for so much of her life that it saddened him. Kevin gave a wonderful eulogy at his funeral, and there was not a person in attendance without tears in his or her eyes. Friends and family set up a foundation in his name, and Burke, McNamara, Sheridan, his brothers, and Jenna would get together at Out of Wack Jack's and reminisce about him. People got over him, as they eventually will, and Connor lost interest in the physical Earth eventually as well. His being was consumed in a gentle darkness, an existence bereft of conflict. He, one with all. A single cell absorbed in all there was and all there will be. Nothing and everything all at once. Peace. Final peace.

BOOKS BY THIS AUTHOR

Fortune And Charge

Live Oak

The Record Of Aesop Vordigan

And, Nothing Himself, Beholds

The Great Dive

ABOUT THE AUTHOR

Matthew Glasgow

Matthew Glasgow is the author of six novels. He also hosts an audio series review and reading of his novels which can be found on Podcast platforms.

Made in the USA
Middletown, DE
06 December 2022

16085515R00085